Eleanor's voice sounded husky. Could she possibly be as affected as he was by their proximity?

Entering her bedroom, Dillon stopped beside the bed, releasing her legs so they dropped until just the tip of her toes were touching the rug. She was just the right height, he realized, oblivious to everything but the woman standing still in his arms.

"You can let me go now," Eleanor said in a hoarse whisper.

"What if I don't want to let you go just yet?" Heating up at the tremor in Eleanor's voice, Dillon wondered exactly what he did want from her.

"You don't really want to do this."

"I don't?" He gulped, her voice splashing like cold water on his growing desire.

"Well, if we do…this, we can't get an annulment."

Dear Reader,

Oh, baby! This June, Silhouette Romance has the perfect poolside reads for you, from babies to royalty, from sexy millionaires to rugged cowboys!

In Carol Grace's *Pregnant by the Boss!* (#1666), champagne and mistletoe lead to a night of passion between Claudia Madison and her handsome boss—but will it end in a lifetime of love? And don't miss the final installment in Marie Ferrarella's crossline miniseries, THE MOM SQUAD, with *Beauty and the Baby* (#1668), about widowed mother-to-be Lori O'Neill and the forbidden feelings she can't deny for her late husband's caring brother!

In Raye Morgan's *Betrothed to the Prince* (#1667), the second in the exciting CATCHING THE CROWN miniseries, a princess goes undercover when an abandoned baby is left in the care of a playboy prince. And some things are truly meant to be, as Carla Cassidy shows us in her incredibly tender SOULMATES series title, *A Gift from the Past* (#1669), about a couple given a surprising second chance at forever.

What happens when a rugged cowboy wins fifty million dollars? According to Debrah Morris, in *Tutoring Tucker* (#1670), he hires a sexy oil heiress to refine his rough-and-tumble ways, and they both get a lesson in love. Then two charity dating-game contestants get the shock of their lives when they discover *Oops...We're Married?* (#1671), by brand-new Silhouette Romance author Susan Lute.

See you next month for more fun-in-the-sun romances!

Happy reading!

Mary-Theresa Hussey

Mary-Theresa Hussey
Senior Editor

Please address questions and book requests to:
Silhouette Reader Service
U.S.: 3010 Walden Ave., P.O. Box 1325, Buffalo, NY 14269
Canadian: P.O. Box 609, Fort Erie, Ont. L2A 5X3

Oops...We're Married?

SUSAN LUTE

SILHOUETTE *Romance*®

Published by Silhouette Books

America's Publisher of Contemporary Romance

To my children,
Darren, Damon and Saritha,
you bring nothing but great joy to my life.
And…
to my husband, David,
I love you.

 SILHOUETTE BOOKS

ISBN 0-373-19671-7

OOPS…WE'RE MARRIED?

Copyright © 2003 by Susan Lute

This edition published by arrangement with Harlequin Books S.A.

® and TM are trademarks of Harlequin Books S.A., used under license.
Trademarks indicated with ® are registered in the United States Patent
and Trademark Office, the Canadian Trade Marks Office and in other
countries.

Visit Silhouette at www.eHarlequin.com

Printed in U.S.A.

SUSAN LUTE

lives in the Pacific Northwest, in the foothills of the Cascade Mountains. She married her high school sweetheart, has three children who are "the best thing she's done with her life" and a dog named Wolfe.

Susan is fascinated by ancient history, loves reading, gardening, black-and-white photographs and traveling. She's a veteran of the Portland to Coast Relay and plans one day to hike the Pacific Crest Trail.

By day she is a registered nurse. By night she loves to spin tales that resemble her own happy-ever-after, about that click of instant recognition that happens when a man and woman fall head over heels in love. When writing, her priorities include that first vanilla latté in the morning and a steady infusion of chocolate.

Dear Reader,

Used to moving from place to place with my family, I was thirteen the summer I discovered a lifelong friend in the guise of a book titled *Black Beauty*. Thus began my career as a reader, which ultimately led to aspirations of becoming a writer. For me, writing about that special, true love is like finally coming home.

I must confess to being an ardent student of human nature. Add a fascination for the ridiculous and the unusual, and you have the conception of Eleanor and Dillon's story. I knew I wanted to explore the relationships between grandparent, parent and child. *Oops...We're Married?* is about widower Dillon Stone and how he reacts when his father and son decide they heartily approve of Eleanor Silks, a corporate librarian so totally opposite from the wife and mother he's decided he has to find.

When I wondered what these two different people would do if they accidentally got married after being thrown together as contestants at a dating-game benefit dinner, their story ran away with me. There's nothing more devastating than love gone horribly wrong, and nothing more heavenly...and satisfying than love when it goes completely right. In the end, only Eleanor and Dillon could tell me how their love would triumph.

In heartfelt appreciation to Silhouette for this opportunity, I give you my first book....

Susan Lute

Prologue

Eleanor Silks Rose sat in the church pew wishing more than anything that it was she standing at the altar becoming Dillon Stone's new wife. It wasn't fair that Joan Butler, Centennial High's sweetheart, with her dark beauty and serene personality, had gotten the most perfect guy in the whole world to walk her down the aisle.

Squirming in pinching panty hose that she rarely put on for any reason, Eleanor watched the ceremony from a seat as far in the back of the small church as she could get and still see down the center aisle to where the couple stood taking their vows. She was oblivious to the soothing music, the serenity of lighted candles and the near tranquillity of the expectant hush as the priest said the words that would join Joan for life to the man Eleanor had secretly loved from the first moment she'd laid eyes on her foster brother Jake's newest friend.

She'd been fourteen then, and still she would give

anything to be in Joan's white patent leather shoes, only Eleanor's choice of elegant footwear ran more to new Nikes than anything shiny or with a heel. To be fair, it wasn't the other woman's fault Dillon had never noticed her, a ragtag tomboy, who would much rather go hiking or follow the boys fishing than do girl things like primp in front of a mirror, clean house, or cook. She would rather eat dirt than do more than pop something frozen into the microwave.

Of course, Joan did all those housewifely things. Tugging on a piece of hair that insisted on curling around her neck, instead of staying in the French braid she'd tried for the first time, Eleanor dropped her gaze as the ceremony ended so she wouldn't see Dillon enthusiastically kissing his new bride.

At the start of the bold music that announced another couple had tied the knot, she looked up to see the happy couple start down the aisle toward her, sparkling in the congratulations of their wedding guests.

Her foster parents were always telling her she had her whole life ahead of her. But, to Eleanor, it sure didn't feel like it.

She refused to cry.

Her heart was not broken.

Another woman had gotten the only man in the world worth considering spending the rest of her life with. King Arthur of Camelot and the Man of Steel all rolled into one, Dillon would always be the only man for her.

Chapter One

"Jake Edward Solomon. You are not my father."

"No, El, but a big brother is the next best thing. Now, are you going to do me this little favor or not?" Jake's voice fairly crackled with humor.

Pushing the phone between her ear and hunched shoulder, Eleanor settled behind her desk and swiveled her chair to gaze unseeing out her office window at the intercity park below.

Jake knew he was going to get his way. Just once, Eleanor wished she could resist her foster brother and one of his crazy schemes. She hated being emotionally blackmailed, especially by the one and only person who came the closest to being any kind of family to her.

"I'm not saying I'll do it, but tell me again what you want me to do?" Eleanor was resigned to helping him out, just like she always did. But, this time, she was determined he was going to have to work hard for his victory.

"The Marshals service is putting on this benefit dinner, and for the price of the ticket we're going to do a dating-game theater show, with a mock marriage at the end—"

"You've got to be kidding, right?" Eleanor knew her voice was on the rise, but at the moment she didn't care as she caught a glimpse of where her foster brother was heading.

"No, I'm not, El. We've got it all arranged for Saturday night, and now one of the girls has backed out."

Eleanor ignored the begging tone Jake tried to trap her with. She'd been exposed to it more times than she cared to remember. In fact, anytime Jake wanted his way.

"I hope you're not suggesting that I should replace this...person in your charade. You know I don't like to do dates...blind, for charity or otherwise," Eleanor reminded Jake flatly, hoping to make him back off.

Wishful thinking.

"Come on, El. I told you I'm in a bind here. I need you. This is very important to a lot of people...and to me."

Eleanor hated it when Jake used his soft, nobody-loves-you-more-than-I-do voice from their teenage years. Emotional blackmail. That's what it was. And, even though it pushed her buttons, she still caved every time.

"Okay, Jake. I'll do this for *you*. I don't care about all those other people. They don't mean a thing to me."

"Of course they don't. Thanks, El. You're a champ and a—"

"Yeah, right," Eleanor broke in, not quite ready to concede the brat his victory.

"Listen," Jake said, "meet me at the Harbor Room tomorrow night and we can go over the details. I'm meeting a friend at five, but we should be done by six. Love you, baby sister."

And then all that was left of Jake and his current mad scheme was the dial tone in Eleanor's ear.

Dillon Stone studied his friend suspiciously in the dim lighting of happy hour at the Harbor Room. Jake couldn't possibly know about his plans to find a wife.

It had been one month since his sister's wedding and his decision to go wife-hunting. And watching Ryan trying to settle into their new home near the university had only strengthened his determination.

Dillon remembered what it had been like after his own mother had died when he was a young teenager—how he'd felt so lost and alone. He'd missed her horribly. He didn't want Ryan to grow up feeling that same loss.

Tangled up in his memories, Dillon wiped away the moisture on the outside of his beer glass with his thumb. He wasn't looking for love for himself. He'd been lucky. He'd had love once. That wasn't something that happened twice in a man's lifetime. The best he could hope for was someone he could respect and live comfortably with. It was doable. Many married for far less.

Dillon thought about the two lists stashed away in his office at home. On one, he'd listed all of the qualities he required in a wife. On the other, all of the single women he thought would fill the bill. Not that the second one was long, but it was a start.

"...so, you can see, I'm kind of in a tight spot here."

"What tight spot?" Dillon lifted his beer to his lips, wincing at having to admit he'd just missed a good portion of his friend's conversation.

"I need a favor. I need a guy Saturday night," Jake spoke slowly as if talking to a slow-witted child, plunking his beer glass on the table between them.

"Sorry, I have a lot on my mind. I've got this involved case I'm reviewing." It wasn't a total lie, Dillon reasoned.

"You don't work in the courts anymore, you're a law professor. What case?"

Dillon had no intention of sharing his latest project with Jake. When the man got ahold of an idea, he was like a dog with a bone. Remembering the number of failed blind dates his buddy had conned him into before he'd started going with Joan at the end of their senior year of high school, he shuddered to think what kind of woman his friend would try to scrounge up for him.

"How's your sister?" Dillon asked, determined to distract Jake.

"El? She's okay. Listen, you have to do this for me—"

For a split second Dillon's stomach churned. Surely, Jake didn't want him to go out with his sister. He remembered the shy tomboy who'd followed them everywhere. If his memory was correct, not long after his marriage to Joan, she'd gone back east to college.

"Do what for you?" he asked cautiously.

"The department is putting on a charity dinner for the East Side Women's Shelter. We'll have a silent auction and some dancing, but most of the program is a mock dating-game theater show, and the guy from the department who was going to be the contestant backed out at the last minute.''

Dillon took a long gulp of his beer, relief flowing down his throat with the malt. His best friend was not setting him up to date his kid sister. The corporate workaholic Jake had said she'd become was not on his agenda. ''What happened to the guy?''

''Got married and his new wife doesn't want him participating.''

''What about one of the other guys?''

''All on assignment, and I'm going to be too busy being master of ceremonies to be a contestant, so don't ask.''

As a U.S. Marshal, Jake took his assignments very seriously, including this one, apparently.

''When is this important 'event'?'' Dillon asked, frowning at the delay to his own plans. He'd just have to work around it. He owed Jake too much. If it hadn't been for his tenacious friend, he didn't know how he would have survived Joan's death.

''This Saturday. I'm sorry this is so last minute, but I'm desperate. And maybe after the show is over, you and the lucky lady you choose can spend some time together.'' An incurable romantic, Jake had already informed Dillon, ad nauseam, that it was about time he rejoined the singles dating scene.

''Not likely, knowing the type of woman you usually rake up for your schemes.'' For a brief moment, Dillon wondered if he was out of his mind to get mixed up in anything his good buddy was involved in.

It's for charity, Stone.

"Okay. I can do it. I guess I'm not doing anything that night, anyway."

"Great." Jake raised his beer in the air. "To success and to finding that perfect woman."

Slowly, Dillon clinked his beer glass to Jake's, suspicion dancing along his nerves. No, Jake couldn't possibly know he was in the market for a new wife. This was just another one his friend's wacky do-gooder schemes.

Finishing his beer, he idly glanced around the dimly lit room until his gaze settled on a woman just entering the lounge. For a breathless moment, with her face half hidden in shadow, she stood motionless, like a priceless porcelain sculpture.

Without his permission and faster than a heartbeat, all Dillon's predatory male instincts came alive. Where in the world did she come from? Interest sneaking up his spine, he couldn't resist feasting on the vision silently taking in the occupants of the room.

Blond hair fell straight past her shoulders like a shimmering pale waterfall, a faint layer of bangs blocked from falling into eyes framed by wire-rimmed glasses. Heart-shaped lips pressed tight in concentration as the woman thoroughly scanned each table, one by one.

Dillon's first thought, *She's looking for someone,* ambushed him into sudden attention as his gaze followed the lithe line of her body. His silent touch moved slowly down her long, slender neck, past proudly held shoulders, then memorized an unforgettable figure that assaulted him with its mounds and valleys—not the least bit hidden by the high-power business suit she wore.

Then the woman stepped farther into the low-lighted room.

Dillon's senses vibrated, like an overstrung guitar string, at the hint of long, lean legs enhanced to perfection by irreverent, practical shoes showcasing fantasy-producing legs and slender feet. Feeling like he'd been gut-kicked, he looked up from his frank appraisal to find the woman staring at him. For a heart-stopping moment, she stood still as if in stunned surprise, then just as quickly dismissed him and flicked her gaze to his friend.

Unaccustomed to being ignored like yesterday's day-old bread, and—God only knew why—not liking it, Dillon watched as the woman's gaze turned suspicious as she started toward their table with undeniable purpose.

His second thought, *Uh-oh, here comes trouble,* settled him back in his chair as he realized there was something familiar about the woman approaching them, anger barely suppressed and certainly not hidden in her smoldering expression.

Dillon's third thought concluded, *This woman is not a Suzie Homemaker.*

"Jake." Eleanor didn't quite succeed in hiding the blazing temper pulsing through her temples behind the cool, even tone of voice she directed at her foster brother. She'd known the brat was up to no good. Here was the proof.

She'd wondered how long it would take Jake to parade her in front of the man she once would have moved heaven and earth for. That childish crush had died a final death on the day he'd married Joan. Though nine years ago she hadn't thought it could be possible, she'd gone on and made something good of her life.

Now, in a nanosecond, she saw everything about Dillon Stone. The faded but well-fitting jeans. The casually worn brown tweed sport coat. Ruffled dark hair that annoyingly begged her fingers to run through it. The sharp, piercing gaze that she was afraid could see to her innermost secrets.

Eleanor ignored the faint tremble in her heart as she felt again his prowling interest when she'd first entered the lounge.

How often had she fought staring at the wedding picture Jake had given her? Each time, pushing down fierce longing for the look of love that radiated from a younger version of this man to another woman, his wife...a dainty, beautiful, dark-haired creature tucked protectively under his arm?

Even though she knew better, for a while she'd looked to find that same love for herself. Finally, convinced she wasn't going to be that lucky, she'd buried the picture and her dream of a true-and-lasting love for herself in the bottom of a box that contained the few mementos she'd somehow saved from her childhood and proceeded to make a successful, independent life for herself that had no room for that unpredictable emotion called love.

"Hey, El." Jake jumped up, his six-foot frame barely towering over her own height of five foot nine as he wrapped her in a strong hug.

Out of the corner of her eye, Eleanor saw Dillon stand, too. Taller than Jake by several inches, his eyes, the color of a deep forest, watched them warily. Then, as if she'd been mistaken, his strong features went carefully blank and the tension riding his hard, lean body visibly disappeared.

Ignoring the sudden awakening of feelings she'd taken great pains to forget, Eleanor pushed at Jake's chest. "Let me go, Jake."

"Fine." Jake's eyes twinkled with mischief as he grabbed the chair next to him in a silent invitation for her to sit. "El, you remember Dillon."

Eleanor shot Jake her most potent I'm-going-to-kill-you-as-soon-as-I-get-you-alone look, then held out her hand to the one man she'd thought never to see again.

"Of course I do." She modulated her voice to cool detachment, strongly shaken by the touch of a handshake that threatened to melt her clear to the center of her soul.

Quickly, she snatched her hand away from his, careful to tuck it behind her back where the man couldn't touch it again.

Green eyes narrowed at her while the sound of Dillon's baritone voice bombarded her with unwanted awareness. "Hi, Eleanor. It's been a long time."

If the look on his face was anything to go by, she was pretty sure he wasn't pleased by this reintroduction. That was just fine with her, Eleanor decided, sinking into the chair Jake offered, her legs not as capable of holding her up as they had been when she'd first entered the lounge. She'd faced many a boardroom piranha and come out the winner since she'd last see this man. She could certainly face down Dillon Stone, who meant nothing to her now, without a single ripple appearing in the well-ordered life she'd intentionally built for herself.

"Jake, I've got to go. I have to get home to Ryan. Eleanor, it was nice to see you again."

Startled, Eleanor watched Dillon's back as he turned and walked away from her, then out the lounge door.

Disappointment pelted her like a cold rainstorm. Obviously, she was as unnoticeable today as she'd been all those years ago when she'd foolishly followed him around wearing her heart on her sleeve.

Slowly, Eleanor turned to Jake. "I think I really am going to kill you this time," she stoically advised her foster brother, painfully aware that her hands had formed into white fists on the table.

Chapter Two

Dillon leaned closer to the mirror, trying to concentrate on the bow tie he was having trouble knotting. It just didn't make any sense. Ever since he'd walked...okay run, away from Eleanor Rose, he hadn't been able to concentrate on a damn thing. Not his preparations for classes. Not his lists. Not anything.

For at least the hundredth time he wondered about her. Her attempt to distance herself hadn't escaped him. He couldn't forget her studied indifference when she'd been forced to acknowledge him.

The woman he'd encountered at the Harbor Room only vaguely resembled the teenage girl Dillon remembered. She'd changed. A lot. The angry tomboy Jake had taken under his wing had morphed into a consummate businesswoman. Too aloof and independent for his tastes, she would never make the cut for his list of potential wife candidates. So, what was his problem?

An attraction for a dyed-in-the-wool corporate businesswoman was not in his plans despite the whiskey-colored eyes haunting him. Or the tall, lithe form and long legs, which he was sure could quite easily wrap themselves around his waist, tempting him. Or the fantasy of sun-struck blond hair cascading through his fingers, taunting him.

A shudder sneaked through Dillon as he savagely clamped down on the runaway images assaulting his good sense. What had happened to the tomboy he used to know?

"Dad. I can't tie this."

Dillon glanced at the reflection of his six-year-old son in the mirrored closet door. Ryan reminded him so much of Joan, bringing back memories of his first wife that no longer hurt, but still left him feeling empty and alone. Though she'd been gone four years, he still missed her laughter and the comfort of coming home to the safety of her love each day.

Turning off the rush of memories he'd worked hard to come to terms with, Dillon squatted down in front of Ryan, quickly tying the boy's bow tie. "You look sharp, champ."

Standing, he turned them both to the mirror. The last of the Stone men, the son a shorter version of his dad, both dressed in black suits, relieved only by white shirts and matching green eyes. One young and too cautious, the other older and sadly wiser.

"Are we going to find a mom tonight?" His son's small voice cut through Dillon's unbidden fantasy of distant, whiskey...blond...

"No. Remember, I told you this is just make-believe. We'll be helping to raise money for—"

"Charity. But I thought as long as you were going to pick a pretend—"

"Pretend," Dillon agreed firmly, wondering if he'd made a mistake including his son in this event.

"I know," Ryan said with a child's aggrieved sigh, then perked up. "Maybe she'll be my pretend mom, too."

Dillon's heart fairly broke at the longing in his little boy's upturned face. He hated that Ryan couldn't remember his mother. In many ways the little guy was so much like her. He had her dark hair, her smile, her easy sense of humor. Even though Ryan had no memory of her, Dillon was aware his son wanted a living mom just like his friends had.

"It's going to be okay, champ. Hey, do you want to help me pick out this pretend wife?" Dillon didn't stop to think before he spoke, but he wouldn't have taken the question back for anything once he saw the excited look that lit up Ryan's face.

"Really?"

"Really." Dillon hoped Jake wouldn't mind a small change in the game plan.

"Do you think we'll find one who really likes us?"

At the wistfulness in his son's voice, Dillon turned them both to look in the mirror one last time.

"Of course she will like us. How could any lady resist two handsome James Bond types like us?" Dillon asked, grateful for the smile his answer put on the little guy's face.

"James Bond."

Dillon watched Ryan square his slight shoulders and once again tug on his tie, before adding in his best imitation James Bond voice, "I'm ready."

That's good, because I'm not sure I am, Dillon acknowledged as he led the way out to his pickup truck.

"This is a great idea, having father-and-son bachelors."

Dillon followed Jake, who led them to the mocked-up booths for the game show. "You're not supposed to see the lady contestants, so sit here and we'll get started as soon as everyone has been served."

"It looks like you have a full house," Dillon observed, glad that if he had to participate in one of Jake's schemes, at least it was for something harmless, but important.

"Yeah, we're packed. We'll make a huge chunk of change for the shelter tonight. I've got to get the ladies settled in their booths. Ryan, sit here next to your dad. You can even ask a question if you want."

"Wow."

Dillon watched Ryan wriggle into the offered chair, relieved that Jake had no problem including his son.

"Wow yourself, little buddy." Ruffling Ryan's hair, Jake pinned on the boy's microphone, then turned laughter-filled eyes toward Dillon. "Good luck. I'm betting you're going to find the perfect woman tonight."

His friend's short laugh, before disappearing around the partition that blocked Dillon's view of the other contestants, filled Dillon with foreboding. Partly because of Jake's recent insistence that he and Ryan needed a change of location, he'd decided to leave Seattle for the smaller, more comfortable Oregon river city of Portland.

Now, he had a familiar feeling his friend was up to no good. He watched as elegantly dressed dinner guests were shown to the tables within his field of vision. "No good" was his buddy's speciality.

"Okay, ladies and gentlemen. It's time to begin," Jake's voice announced. "Let me start out by thanking each of you for coming tonight to help support this very worthy cause. Remember, at the back of the room is a silent auction. All proceeds made tonight will go directly to the East Side Women's Shelter...."

Maybe his friend was right. There were three eligible women on the other side of the wall that separated him and Ryan from them. One of the ladies could be just what he was looking for...an addition to the list he'd left safely at home.

"For a surprise addition, we have not one bachelor, but two very eligible bachelors, father and son, who will pick a very lucky bachelorette...."

Eleanor stopped squirming in the hard chair Jake had shown her to, suspicion splashing her with a cold panic that was rapidly turning to anger.

He wouldn't. The one person in the whole world she trusted, wouldn't do this to her, would he? Yes...he would, a small voice offered its opinion in her mind. Eleanor spit silent curses at her brother. The three-sided cubicle where she sat, unable to lay her hands on him, revealed only an excited audience, beginning their dinner as they eagerly waited for the "dating game" to begin.

"Bachelor senior. Why don't you start with your first question. We have three lovely ladies for you to choose from. Will it be Bachelorette number one? Bachelorette number two? Or Bachelorette number three?''

''Bachelorette number three. What are your hobbies?''

Eleanor almost groaned aloud when she heard the unforgettable, familiar voice ask his first question amid cheers and catcalls from the audience. She wasn't prepared for the deep impact of his voice that ignited undisciplined awareness like Fourth of July fireworks.

''Bachelorette number three?'' Dillon's dark, gravelly voice washed her in unexplained waves of startled sensation.

Clearing the lump suddenly lodged in her throat, Eleanor blurted without thinking, ''I don't have any hobbies.''

''I see. How about Bachelorette number two?''

What did he see? Eleanor wondered angrily, feeling both foolish and irritated. Only what she wanted him to see. Which was nothing.

The honey tones used by the other two ladies to answer the law professor's question made Eleanor sick to her stomach. There was no way she was going to try to sell herself to this man by sugarcoating her responses just for his benefit.

''Bachelorette number three. What are your favorite foods?''

This time Eleanor was prepared. Carefully modulating her voice, she responded, ''I'm a vegetarian.'' Well, she was.

''And...?''

''And, I like vegetables.''

Dillon looked at Ryan, his eyebrows lifting in

question. There was something familiar about that
voice, even though it was masked by the microphone
and her abrupt responses.

Briefly, whiskey-colored eyes flashed bright in
Dillon's mind and the last puzzle piece fell into
place. So, that's what all Jake's meddling was about.
He had three ladies to choose from. Of course, he
wasn't going to pick Eleanor just because she was
Jake's sister. The guy could be a loose cannon, but
this little maneuver absolutely took the cake.

Eleanor stared out at the audience. The dinner was
being catered by attendants dressed sharply in white
shirts, black bow ties and black dress slacks. The
tables were elegantly covered in gold tablecloths.
And, without exception, every female eye in the
place was focused on the left side of the stage, where
she was sure Dillon sat with his little boy.

Heated with disgust, she unbuttoned the top button of the white blouse that seemed bent on choking
her and renewed her earlier vow not to stoop to
competing for the man's attention. Purposely, she
answered each question Dillon asked her in the most
bored, disinterested way she could, discouraging
any idea the man might have of picking her, while
the other ladies blatantly threw themselves at him.
Their sugary, come-park-your-shoes-under-my-bed
responses made her stomach queasy.

When Jake stepped into her line of vision, frowning at her, Eleanor felt a small pinpoint of malicious
satisfaction. She arched her eyebrows at him, smiled
sweetly and wished him at the bottom of the Pacific
Ocean. It warmed her sense of revenge when his
frown deepened.

If she could just get to him, she would really hurt

Jake, Eleanor promised, finding herself perched on
the edge of her seat, leaning out of the small cubicle
that marked her end of the stage.

Pushing her glasses farther up her nose, she briefly
glanced toward the other end of the raised platform.
Three additional cubicles, undoubtedly perfect matches
to hers, stretched across the stage in a half moon, the
two middle ones recessed slightly away from the audience. Suddenly, Eleanor found herself traitorously
wondering what it would be like to be chosen by Dillon
Stone. What would it be like to be the woman he would
want to spend the rest of his life with?

Before she could break away from that heart-
pounding thought, a solemn face peeked around the
front of the bachelor cubicle. Serious eyes studied
her without blinking. A sudden smile shattered the
illusion of an adult packed secretly into the small
boy's body.

Ryan.

The longing in his watchful eyes assailed Eleanor
with an unfamiliar urge to take the small, serious
child and fold him close in her arms. Tentatively, she
smiled back.

"Bachelorette number three?" Dillon's annoyed
voice broke the fragile connection she'd made with
the child.

"I'm sorry. I didn't hear the question," she said
as she removed her glasses and winked at Ryan, who
was still watching her curiously.

"Where is your favorite place to vacation?" Dillon repeated, patience struggling with the irritation
lacing his voice.

"I don't go on vacation," Eleanor answered truthfully, her mind still on a little boy's heartbreaking smile as she scooted back into the uncomfortable chair.

"Okay..." The increasingly frustrated voice plowed through her thoughts. For the first time since she'd started this nightmare, Eleanor relaxed. For a second, she thought she could hear the man grinding his teeth. She smiled.

"Ryan. Come sit down," Dillon whispered to his son, amazed at how hard it was to hide his frustration with Eleanor's answers. He didn't really care what they were, and he certainly wasn't planning to choose her for his "pretend" wife, but the woman could at least make some attempt at being interested in the game; for the audience's sake if nothing else.

Pushing away the image of whiskey-colored eyes and a body that promised to be a perfect match to his in the intricate dance of love, he helped Ryan climb back into his seat. He wasn't interested in love, and it was with irritating effort that he finally wiped the seductive image from his mind.

"Okay. Bachelor junior. You get to ask the last question." Jake's booming voice broke into Dillon's annoyance.

"James Bond," Dillon reminded his son softly.

"Bachelor three. Do you like kids?" At the small quiver in Ryan's voice, Dillon placed his arm around his son's shoulders.

Eleanor heard the loneliness in the child's voice and understood it completely. She couldn't stop herself from remembering how his grown-up study had changed so quickly to a child's curiosity with one beautiful smile. Without further thought, she answered truthfully, from her heart, unable to cause more hurt to the little person who'd silently reached out to her.

"I think...kids are cool...especially little boys," she said hesitantly, but simply.

Surprised at the sudden warmth in Eleanor's voice, Dillon watched a smile spread over his son's face. He didn't really listen to the other two bachelorette's responses, although chatty number two had the three of them at Chuck E. Cheese's long before she was done.

How could the woman who'd answered so warmly to Ryan be the same woman who had been evasive, impersonal and dismissive with him all evening?

As a slow anger began to burn in his throat, Dillon flicked his finger at a piece of lint on his jacket sleeve. Even though he considered himself an average sort of guy, he wasn't used to being treated like a pariah by women. Dillon reluctantly admitted he didn't like it. It didn't matter that he wasn't planning on picking Eleanor. It was just that she could at least play nice.

"All right, ladies and gentlemen. It's time for our bachelors to choose their bachelorette." Jake's voice floated over the audio system, reminding Dillon that fortunately this whole nonsense would soon be over.

"Okay, Ryan. Which one do we want? Bachelorette number one or number two?" Dillon whispered to his son as if asking the boy to help him pick between his two least favorite desserts.

"We want Bachelorette three." Ryan's excited answer caused blaring alarms to clang loudly in Dillon's head.

"No, Ryan. We need to pick either one or two." There was no way he was going to pick Eleanor Rose after her obvious lack of interest throughout the whole game. It was only a benefit dinner, for God's sake. The woman could have at least tried to pretend she wanted to participate.

"But I want Bachelorette three." Ryan's hands were balling into fists, his voice changing from a whisper to sharp demand.

"Ryan," Dillon insisted firmly, pulling the resisting boy against his chest.

"But I want her to be my new mom." The shake in Ryan's voice and the tears flooding his eyes was more than Dillon had the strength to fight, but he tried, anyway.

"This is just pretend, son. And only for tonight. Okay?"

"Okay. But, I still want Bachelorette three."

At that moment Jake rounded the corner into the cubicle and caught the tail end of their discussion. Dillon groaned inwardly at his buddy's apparent amusement at his predicament.

"It appears our bachelors are having a difference of opinion over which bachelorette they want," Jake said, playing to the expectant audience for all he was worth.

A burst of chatter erupted, forcing Dillon's hand. Resigned to his fate, he stood, taking Ryan up in his arms, anchoring his son's light weight on his hip. As he faced the excited audience, a breathless hush replaced the noisy chatter.

"We'll take Bachelorette number...three," he said on a reluctant sigh.

Thank God it was just pretend and just for the night, he told himself. He was a big boy. He could put up with Eleanor Rose for one night. The smile that spread across his son's face and his little hands clapping gleefully amid thundering applause from the audience was all the confirmation he needed that he'd made the right choice...for his son.

Dillon thanked Bachelorettes number one and two, speculatively watching number two leave the stage. Her backward look was full of promise, if he'd only take her up on the offer. Mary Towers was her name. She was definitely the Suzie Homemaker type he was looking for and appeared to like kids just fine. Maybe he would add her to his list of possibilities.

She's just what I'm looking for. She'd make a great mother for Ryan, he was thinking when his gaze collided with angry, storm-filled, whiskey eyes that reminded him of...

Then it was just the four of them left on the stage. Ryan, his smile big, his eyes bright with excitement. Jake, grinning with smug satisfaction. Eleanor, her face white, her lips pressed into a thin, painful-looking line, her expressive eyes swimming with an emotion he couldn't put a name to. And himself.

Dillon didn't like the laughter that tinted Jake's voice when he turned to the audience. ''Ladies and gentlemen. May I introduce Portland's hottest new couple, Dillon Stone and Eleanor Rose.''

Flicking his gaze from his son's excited grin to Jake's triumphant laughter, then to Eleanor Rose's disbelieving stillness, Dillon couldn't shake the sinking feeling that instead of being almost over, this night's high jinks were only just beginning.

Chapter Three

"Ladies and gentlemen. We're going to have a short intermission while we set up the wedding scene. Don't forget to take a look at the silent auction at the back of the room."

Eleanor wanted to scream at the top of her lungs at the turn Jake's so-called "dating game" had taken. Hastily she tugged her foster brother away from Dillon's frown and the excitement dancing in his little boy's eyes.

"Jake. I am not going to marry that…man," she whispered fiercely, turning her back on the tantalizing promise Dillon Stone represented.

"Of course you are. It's perfectly safe, all make-believe. For charity, remember?"

Eleanor shook off Jake's arm when he tried to wrap her in a smothering hug.

"He should have picked one of the others. Why didn't he?" Eleanor didn't like the feeling that she was losing it.

"Because you're so sweet and wonderful? And, he couldn't resist you?" Humor played across Jake's face, only inching her irritation higher.

"You're dead meat."

"Thanks, El. I love you, too. Look out, here come the wedding props."

Intent on getting as far away from Dillon Stone and his sweet little boy as she possibly could, Eleanor scowled her worst at Jake before moving out of the way of the stage workers who were exchanging the cubicles for an elaborate garden wedding scene.

"This isn't going to work, you know," Dillon told his friend evenly, while Jake fixed the bridal boutonniere in his jacket lapel. Covertly, he watched Eleanor across the stage, fidgeting tensely while a woman, presumably one of Jake's assistants, placed a long, trailing, lacy veil over her flowing blond hair.

God, she was beautiful. She certainly wasn't a shy tomboy anymore. Gone was the young girl he remembered. In her place was a gorgeous woman, but one who still lacked all the female graces.

"Sure, it's going to work. The crowd loves this stuff." Jake indicated the wedding arch that was being placed center stage.

"No. I mean Eleanor and me." Dillon didn't believe the picture that was being created of Eleanor as the perfect bride. Unexpectedly, a painful knot formed in his stomach at the fleeting, wistful look she cast at him. A look that was concealed behind indifference before it was ever fully formed.

Damn. Why was he even thinking about this? He wanted more children. Maybe, lots of them. And in his experience, career women did not want children.

At least not right away. Anyone could see that Eleanor Rose was a dedicated career woman.

Even now, she was dressed in a gray pin-striped skirt and jacket as if she couldn't wait to get back to the office. Surprisingly, the top button of her blouse was open, exposing a generous amount of her slender throat, slightly spoiling her perfect corporate image. But that didn't change the fact that he'd met her type before.

"What about you and Eleanor?" Jake's pseudo-innocent inquiry made the hairs stand at alert on the back of Dillon's neck.

"We have absolutely nothing in common. After tonight we'll probably never see each other again." The ping that poked his heart at the thought of never seeing Eleanor again didn't mean a thing. Suspiciously, Dillon watched his friend's unchanging expression. Mary Towers was the more obvious choice for his list of possible wife candidates.

"Hey. No problem. But it wouldn't hurt if you and El got together after this."

Get together? With Eleanor Rose? The poster lady of corporate womanhood? No way.

"It's not going to happen, Jake," Dillon firmly informed his friend.

"All I'm saying—"

"Dad, how come she's standing way over there?" Ryan pulled insistently on his hand, effectively derailing Dillon's conversation with Jake—a conversation that had been going nowhere, anyway.

"Because the bride and groom are not supposed to see each other before the wedding ceremony, pal." Jake answered for him, dropping on one knee to fix a matching boutonniere on Ryan's lapel. "Everything seems to be ready. Why don't we get your dad and El in place?''

Eleanor turned to face the man she'd worked so hard to keep out of her dreams. She couldn't go through with this. She wasn't going to pretend to marry the one man who had once had the power to rock her to her very soul.

''El, come stand over here.''

Jake's instruction set her teeth on edge. Forcing stiff limbs to move, Eleanor slowly walked to the spot her foster brother indicated.

Why was she doing this? Because it was a fake ceremony...and for charity. Eleanor squared her shoulders. She had a fulfilling career and was just fine living on her own. She was not feeling sorry for herself or wishing for the impossible just because as a young woman she'd once wished she could be bound to this man for life.

A small hand nestled into hers. Unable to stop the feelings suddenly warming her, Eleanor looked down into shining green eyes and the biggest smile she'd ever seen on a child's face.

''You're going to be my new mom,'' Ryan said, eyes twinkling at her. Eleanor's heart sank. She didn't need any new cracks to form in her armor.

''Remember, son, this is just make-believe.'' Dillon's determined words sealed those cracks shut with a lonely clang.

''Where's the judge? Is there a judge in the house?'' Jake demanded playfully of the audience.

In unison the audience began to loudly chant. ''Judge...judge...judge...''

Keep your sense of humor. Don't break your heart over this, Eleanor admonished herself as a sprinkle of laughter drifted through the room. Nervously, she adjusted her glasses on her nose. This mockery of a marriage was for charity. It didn't mean anything more than that.

Taking a deep breath to settle the skittish alarm clanging in her stomach, Eleanor looked up as a new disturbance erupted at the door. Now what?

Causing the minor commotion was an elderly man in a western-style black frock and flat-brimmed black hat. Haphazardly, he was making his way toward the stage, patting his pockets as if he'd lost something. Finally, out of one deep side pocket, he pulled out wire-rimmed spectacles and pushed them onto his bulbous nose.

"So sorry I'm late," the old man wheezed, out of breath as he stopped opposite Dillon.

Eleanor couldn't believe her eyes. Jake couldn't have gotten a more disreputable-looking judge if he'd tried, which he probably had, she decided, disgusted. The man looked as if he'd been pulled right out of an old-time western.

"Are you two young folks ready? I'm Jed Banta. This is my third wedding for the day and I'd like to get started," the old man muttered as Jake attached a microphone to his once starched collar.

"Okay, young fella, what's your name?"

Dillon couldn't help smiling at the old man's appearance. Where in the world had Jake found this decrepit old gent? He was perfect for the part of an old boomtown judge. Even down to the unkempt white hair poking out from beneath the wide brim of his felt hat and the thick white mustache that generously covered his lips.

"Uh...I'm Dillon Stone." Dillon choked back a

chuckle as the old man licked the end of a stubby pencil, then wrote his name on a slip of paper he'd pulled from the inside pocket of his coat.

The man's act was perfect, Dillon realized, as the audience openly responded to his antics.

"Miss? What's your name?"

For a moment Dillon thought Eleanor wouldn't go along. Her face was as white as the paper the judge was poised over, and he was sure she was about to faint. What was she afraid of? Because from where he stood, Eleanor Rose was definitely afraid.

When he'd been a criminal lawyer, he'd seen the same look of sick fear on many a defendant's face just before the verdict came down. Slowly, he laced his fingers with hers and was shocked by the bolt of electricity that raced from their touching hands clear down to curl his toes.

"Eleanor?" he prodded. Had she felt that electric zing, too?

Her pale face flushed with a pretty blush as she turned to look at him. The surprised look darkening her remarkable eyes heated the sizzle that was still blistering his fingertips.

"My name..." Finally she looked away, leaving Dillon with an uneasy feeling there was something important he was missing.

"Eleanor Rose Silks. My name is Eleanor Silks Rose."

That brief moment of vulnerable emotion caused strange feelings of protectiveness to quicken Dillon's heartbeat. The woman was so filled with contradictions. It didn't make sense that he didn't want to let her go when she pulled away from their connecting touch.

"Well, let's get started," the old man said. "We are gathered here…"

Eleanor was still trying to catch her breath from that moment when Dillon had held her hand. She'd been feeling so chilled, thinking about pretending to do something she would have given her right arm to do for real when she was nineteen.

But, of course, she didn't want to marry Dillon Stone now. She'd made a perfect life for herself, resigned that her knight on a white charger had already been taken and his twin was not to be found anywhere. Then he'd intertwined his fingers with hers and consuming heat and hunger had licked at a loneliness she hadn't known she'd lived with for too long.

Still reeling from the warm embers that scorched her, Eleanor looked up into her foster brother's sympathetic smile. Before she could throw the tantrum she was thinking of and stick out her tongue at him, mischief-filled eyes dared her to go through with this farce of a pretend marriage.

Eleanor swallowed the fear crowding her throat. Her gaze moved from Jake's satisfied expression to little Ryan's equally excited face. Something long buried stirred near her bruised heart. How could she protect herself when such a sweet little boy persisted in staring at her with stars in his eyes? Eyes that exactly matched the older, more experienced ones of his father.

"Do you, Dillon Stone, take Eleanor Rose to be your wife, to love and to cherish, as long as you both shall live?"

Dillon's deep "I do" made a pair of excited shivers somersault up Eleanor's spine as she locked gazes with the man standing so calmly at her side. What was he thinking? Frantically, she fought a bubble of hysteria.

"Do you, Eleanor Rose, take Dillon Stone to be your husband, to love and to cherish, as long as you both shall live?" Unbidden, a very secret part of her heart surprised her with the wish that she could love and cherish Dillon, and that he would love and cherish her, for longer than the rest of their lives.

"I..." Eleanor cleared her throat. *This is for charity*. She tried again. "I do," she whispered.

"I now pronounce you husband and wife. Young man, you may kiss your bride." The judge's pronouncement stretched Eleanor's sense of the unreal.

"No," she objected in a croaked whisper, earning a frown from Dillon that stopped her in her tracks. She didn't like the sudden glint of determination that lit his searching green eyes.

Realizing his intent, Eleanor turned her head at the last minute so that his warm lips landed on the corner of hers. Instead of quickly kissing, then releasing her immediately, he tantalizingly stayed there a second too long...lingering...testing...nibbling...seducing.

Stunned by the feeling of his lips exploring her sensitive skin, Eleanor forced herself to push against the hard landscape of his chest. Somehow, she had to resist the feelings tumbling through her stomach and the heat attempting to warm her skin. Closing her heart off to any more temptation, she stepped back from Dillon, only to find his hands firmly clamped at her waist, preventing her escape.

"Here. If you young people will sign this, we'll be all done." Amid cheers from the audience,

Eleanor watched Dillon sign the phony license, then added her name below his bold scrawl.

"How about a big round of applause for our winners." Jake was at the microphone again. "Let's see if we can get our newest couple to lead us in a dance. Come on, everyone. Let's give them some encouragement."

Dillon glanced at Eleanor, surprised by the panicked look that spread over her classic features, as the swell of goodwill and rhythmic clapping grew around them. Still stunned by the raw feelings racing through him from the brief brush of his lips across hers and the firm feel of her waist between his hands, he wondered what was going on in the woman's head.

He thought about the vulnerability that occasionally flickered across Eleanor's lovely face, the loneliness she tried so hard to hide. The unmistakably sensual way she moved pulled at Dillon despite his best efforts to ignore the alarming fireworks that went off every time he got too close to the woman. The way he was now.

As the demand of the dinner guests grew, he watched Eleanor struggle to recapture the cool reserve that pricked his normally nonexistent temper. What was wrong with her that she couldn't relax and just go with the flow for the evening?

Frowning, Dillon decided he was going to have a talk with his friend. Jake shouldn't have put his sister in such an uncomfortable position. He suspected his buddy had his own reasons for maneuvering them both into being here…together. But it wasn't right.

"Let's dance. It's the only way we'll get them to

leave us alone.'' Expressive eyes darted to Dillon's, anger darkening them to a shuttered brown.

"Come on. I won't bite,'' he offered in reassurance, even as her tension sneaked into his body by way of the hand he'd never moved from the small of her straight back. Briefly, she leaned into his shoulder, causing annoying waves of hard-hitting awareness to leap through him. Then her back became rigid again, her delicate features wearing a careful, blank mask.

"Sure.'' Eleanor couldn't believe she'd almost melted into Dillon's arms when the expression on his handsome face changed to bewildering concern.

She lifted her chin and sealed her heart. How long could one measly slow dance last, anyway? As Dillon pulled her close, his touch ignited unwanted tremors of excitement that began in her belly and spiraled out of control to the rest of her suddenly alert body. There was only one thing left to do. She had to take this bull by the horns and toss him out of her corral as soon as possible.

"So, what made you decide to pick me? Weren't the other two ladies more to your liking?''

"They were. I didn't pick you. Ryan did.'' Dillon couldn't bite his tongue quick enough to stop the rude words, peeved that the woman had maneuvered him into being so juvenile. When this dance was over he and Ryan were out of here as soon as he could make it happen.

"Do you always let your son pick your dates for you?''

Dillon didn't miss the angry flush that spread over Eleanor's porcelain skin or the way his body responded to the slender form he held close to him. If he wasn't careful, the wasp would realize she ignited more than his temper.

"This isn't really a date, so I figured this time it wouldn't matter." Whirling Eleanor to the tempo of the music, Dillon got tangled in the vanilla fragrance he'd noticed earlier when he'd kissed the stiff woman in his arms.

Telling himself he was not going to give in to the overwhelming desire to smell her long hair, Dillon stepped back slightly to escape the irresistible entrapment she seemed to weave around him.

Fortunately, Eleanor didn't notice his withdrawal. She was too busy ignoring him...and watching Ryan, who was eating an ice-cream sundae with Jake and the fake judge. A rare expression softened her features. How could she be as prickly as a cactus one minute and soft with unspoken longing the next?

Before Dillon could pursue that thought, Eleanor muttered, "Now, what's he up to?"

"Who?" But he already knew the answer as he saw one of Jake's fellow U.S. Marshals lean close to his friend's shoulder. Jake nodded briskly, changing instantly from the laughing mischief-maker he usually portrayed to the no-nonsense U.S. Deputy Marshal he really was.

"Looks like maybe we're done here," Dillon said cheerfully as he and Eleanor walked to the table where Jake was now standing.

"What's up?" Dillon pulled a chair out for Eleanor to sit next to Ryan.

"I just got the orders I've been waiting for on a case I was assigned last week. I have just enough time to pack a bag and turn my house keys over to a friend I'm subletting to."

"You're subletting your house? To whom?" Dillon watched Ryan climb down from his chair to stand close to Eleanor's shoulder as he seriously studied her. He was afraid to guess what was going through his son's agile mind.

"Remember my buddy who just got married? Well, the closing on their house got delayed and their lease ran out, so he and the new wife are going to stay at my place until the deal on their house closes."

Dillon knew better, but he asked, anyway. "Where are you going?"

Jake only shrugged his shoulders and smiled his most secret grin, not about to give anything away.

"You're my new mom, aren't you?"

Dillon glanced quickly at his son and groaned. Once the little guy got something stuck in his mind, it was so hard to convince him otherwise.

"Son, remember this is only make-believe. Eleanor and I didn't really get married tonight—"

Suddenly spitting into his napkin, the fake judge jumped up from his seat. "What do you mean you're not married? Of course you're married. I just married you in front of God and witnesses."

Dillon laughed. "You're kidding, right?"

"No."

Stunned, Dillon looked from the old guy to his excited son, then noticed the horrified look on Eleanor's frozen features.

"No. This can't be real," she whispered, one elegant hand going to the frantically beating pulse at her throat.

Unable to believe what he was hearing, Dillon

looked at Jake, suspicion starting to crawl up his spine as a delighted smile spread across his friend's face.

"Yes, ma'am. I married ya. As a duly appointed judge in the State of Oregon, I've been marrying folks for nigh on forty years. Can't think why it wouldn't be legal now. You young folks signed the license, all right. We had witnesses. And I signed, too. That's how it's done." Pulling his spectacles from his nose, the old gent squinted while he gingerly wiped the glasses with a snowy-white hankie he pulled from his breast pocket.

Legally married to Eleanor Rose? But she's not even on my list.... She's not what I'm looking for, was all Dillon could think. Freezing mid-thought, he glared at his good buddy.

Barely suppressing a desire to punch him in the shoulder the way she did when they were kids and he'd gotten her into one more mess, Eleanor hissed at Jake. "You did this."

"No, I didn't. I swear it. I wish I had." Jake backed away, holding his hands up, palms toward her in surrender, his voice filled with as much surprise as she felt. "I admit, I did work to get you both here, but even I wouldn't have the guts to deliberately plan a secret marriage between the two of you."

"Then how did this happen?" Eleanor fired back at her foster brother, horrified to find tears gathering behind her eyes before the thought of murdering Jake rescued her.

"Maybe Cupid had something to do with it," Jake offered, his expression suddenly soft with caring, before changing to pleased approval as he continued his retreat, his hands still lifted in total surrender.

Cupid? Did the brat have any brain cells left at all?

"Jake Solomon, don't you dare leave now. You have to fix this. I can't be married to him." Eleanor watched her foster brother's expression change to naughty-boy mischief, and her heart sank.

"I can't stay, El. I've got an assignment. I have to leave. I'm sorry. I can't fix this for you. Dillon will have to take care of everything. But if you want to know my opinion, I think this is the best thing to ever happen. I only wish I could claim responsibility, so I could take the credit and hold it over your heads for the rest of your lives."

With a quick wave, a deep chuckle of delight and the parting words, "Dillon, take care of El for me, she's very special," Jake was gone, leaving Eleanor feeling very frustrated and suddenly more alone than ever.

Eleanor turned slowly, her mind working at top speed for a way out of the bizarre predicament Jake had left her in. Dillon and Ryan waited behind her; Dillon warily, Ryan not containing his wild excitement.

"Where's that judge? We have to talk to him, get him to undo this, make us unmarried or something." Eleanor couldn't stop the panic that edged her babbling.

"He's gone," Dillon said. "Couldn't stop him. Said he had another wedding to perform." Still feeling as if his wits had been scrambled, he clutched their wedding license in one hand and Ryan's hand in the other. "And, by the looks of this paper, unless I can find a loophole, I'd say we are legally married."

Chapter Four

Dillon shifted uneasily at the smothering tension that surrounded them as he, Ryan and Eleanor climbed into his pickup. Once Ryan heard that his dad and Eleanor were really married, his son had latched on to Eleanor's hand as if he was never going to let the woman go.

Even now, Ryan was leaning forward from the back seat of the extended cab, his tiny hand resting possessively on Eleanor's shoulder. In a brief movement, she shifted, trapping his son's fingers between her shoulder and ear. Gently, she moved her head back and forth as if she was trying to smooth away some disappointment she knew was coming.

Sudden desire streaked through Dillon at the surprising gesture. Did Eleanor care for his son's tender feelings? She probably didn't have a clue how attractive that possibility made her.

"Ryan, sit back and put your seat belt on." Dillon turned the key to start the engine, still thinking about the seemingly distant woman beside him. Her classic features carefully blank, Eleanor turned away from him, looking into the still night outside her window.

"I can't believe Jake left me without a ride home," she mumbled unhappily.

"What do you want to do now?" he asked a little gruffly, unreasonably wanting to shatter her isolation.

"I want to go home."

"You're going home with us. You're my new mom."

The enthusiasm in Ryan's little voice sparkled brightly, filling Dillon with regret and anger. Ryan deserved to have a mom. A real mom, not this silent, remote, accidental "mom" who'd gently rubbed her cheek against his son's small hand before the child reluctantly sat back and fastened his seat belt.

"Ryan, Miss Eleanor and I are not really married," Dillon gently reminded his son as Eleanor's stiff posture made him wonder angrily what was really going on behind the silent mask of her features. For a moment, while they'd danced, she'd taken her glasses off, but now they were firmly back in place, a shield she apparently hid behind. "There was a mistake. She doesn't want to come home with us."

When Eleanor swung around to glare at him, her silky blond hair swinging wildly around her shoulders, he realized he'd chosen the wrong words. And it made him even angrier. It wasn't his fault she didn't want to be married to him. He didn't want to be married to her, either. And, just for that brief second, crawling out from under some hidden rock in his soul was a feeling of confusing disappointment.

"The man said he married you. That means she's my mom."

In a heartbeat, the wildfire in the deep whisky eyes hiding behind the windows of her glasses, changed to disbelieving panic, matching the feeling starting to fuel Dillon's own emotions.

"We can't possibly be married. We didn't even have blood tests." Eleanor took a deep breath, trying not to show her rising panic. How had she let herself get into this predicament? She was always so careful. If you controlled your life and didn't allow anyone too close, then you couldn't get hurt. Ever.

She knew this the same way she knew her hair was blond and her eyes that strange, clear brown color. Where had she gone wrong? Without her permission, drop-dead gorgeous Dillon Stone had gotten through her door like the wolf in Little Red Riding Hood.

She was going to kill Jake. She'd probably have to go to jail for the deed, but it would be worth it. The small spark of satisfied revenge slightly eased her unstable feelings.

"You don't have to have blood tests to get married in Oregon."

Dillon's deep voice interrupted her plans for retaliation, forcing Eleanor to really look at the man for the first time since she'd realized they could actually be legally bound for life, making one of her most secret fantasies come true. "Are you sure?"

"Yes."

Eleanor didn't like the speculation sparkling in eyes that saw more than she wanted them to. Though he was older than her memory of him, he was only more handsome, more exciting, more...sexy now than he was when she'd trailed him like a lovesick puppy.

"I want to go home. To my home."

"I want you to go home with us."

Eleanor turned at the tears surfacing in Ryan's voice. Her heart lurched at the emotion pouring from the little guy, and in that second, he slipped past her defenses, into her fragile heart. Trying to shore up the crumbling walls, with Ryan looking at her, his whole heart in his eyes, was nearly impossible. But, for her own safety, she had to.

"I can't come to your house tonight," she told him gently.

"But—"

"Ryan..." Dillon's troubled voice interrupted his son's heartfelt plea.

"How about if I come see you tomorrow?" Eleanor held her breath, hoping a short visit would satisfy the child.

He looked down and his little lip trembled. Eleanor's heart tore when he finally agreed with a quivering, "Okay."

Terrified, she realized this was not going to work. She couldn't possibly be a wife and a mother...all at the stroke of a mistaken "I do."

Dillon sat at his desk in the study, holding the two pieces of paper that contained his lists—one, the list of the important characteristics he wanted in a wife; the other, the short list of possible candidates.

Fate was playing a joke on him. Nowhere did he find Eleanor Rose listed or even remotely indicated by a single wanted attribute. What had gone wrong with his plan?

Dillon rubbed his eyes, wishing he could wipe away more than his tiredness. He'd barely slept last night. Each time he'd woken up, it was to dreams of creamy, porcelain skin, long, enticing legs, dreamy whiskey eyes and luscious heart-shaped lips. Lips begging for his kiss.

The woman wasn't even his type. Why was he dreaming and thinking about her like some randy teenager? His sister, Beth, would suggest his dreams meant something, but he disagreed.

They could mean you're undeniably attracted to your new wife.

Stunned at the thought, Dillon looked up to find Ryan standing in the doorway, steadily watching him with his too solemn expression.

Pushing his delinquent thoughts to the darkest corner of his mind—where maybe they would get lost—Dillon beckoned, "Come sit on my lap, son."

Once Ryan was settled, Dillon ached when green eyes, round with worry, settled on him as his child grabbed his face with both hands.

"Are you tired, Dad?"

"Yes, I am a little. I didn't sleep very well last night." Dillon hugged Ryan close. His son was the most important thing in his life. That would never change.

"I didn't, either."

Sometimes, life played funny tricks on you. He'd heard about the child becoming the parent and the parent becoming the child, but never believed it until that moment.

"Don't you like Miss Eleanor? She'd make a good wife," the little boy stated in his curiously grown-up voice.

She's already my wife.

"Maybe. But it takes a lot more than accidentally

getting married to make a good marriage,'' he replied, holding Ryan back to get a better look at the thoughtful frown on his son's face.

"Can't you just like her the way she is? That's what you tell me to do,'' Ryan said, the crease taking over the space between his little brows.

"Well, it's not that simple. To be married, two people should have things in common. Important things like wanting to have kids or liking the same foods or wanting to go to the zoo together.'' Dillon grappled with his son's question as he leaned back in his chair, gently rubbing the skin between the boy's brows, determined to erase the lingering frown.

"Miss Eleanor likes kids. She told me so. She likes vegetables. We eat *our* vegetables. I don't know if she likes to go to the zoo, but I can ask her. We should keep her.''

"I don't think she wants us to 'keep her,' son.''

Dillon glanced at the book on his desk and thought of the lists tucked away in its pages. As far as he could tell Eleanor did not match up with any of the characteristics that he required in a wife. He didn't want a woman who was not the Suzie Homemaker he was looking for. He knew it was an old-fashioned concept, having a stay-at-home wife, which put him in the dubious category of being a chauvinist, but he had to consider Ryan's needs. Besides, Eleanor didn't want to be with him, either.

How was he going to explain all this to a six-year-old? It wasn't a conversation an adult usually had with their child. The jarring ring of the doorbell launched the little boy off Dillon's lap, saving him at the last minute.

"She's here!" he shouted excitedly, running out of the room to answer the door.

Dillon followed more slowly, uncomfortable with the thoughts spinning through his mind like an out-of-control circus ride. It couldn't work. They were too opposite. Then he remembered the wistful-ness...the vulnerability peeking out before she could hide it last night, and he started to wonder...

By the time he got to the front door, Ryan, talking a mile a minute, had a bemused-looking Eleanor Rose by the hand, pulling her into the house.

"—glad you're here. I want to show you my bed-room and my toys. Do you like pizza or going to the zoo? They're my favorite things. Will you make cookies, with me? You do know how to make cook-ies don't you? If you don't, I can show—"

"Hold on there, bud, you're scaring Miss Eleanor. Let's take her to the living room and give her a chance to catch her breath," Dillon suggested, inter-rupting his son's high-speed demands, afraid of where the little guy might be going with his endless questions.

Despite the longing in her eyes when she looked at Ryan, Eleanor looked about as comfortable as she would be if she'd accidentally walked into a lion's den. Maybe she had, Dillon conceded.

Eleanor allowed herself to be directed to the spa-cious living room. Her mind occupied with her new dilemma, she wasn't really paying attention to Ryan's mile-a-minute one-sided conversation.

She hadn't slept much last night. When she'd fi-nally gotten home, it was to find a message on her voice mail, telling her the sweet Cape Cod she'd rented for the last six months had been sold. She had to be out by Friday or her landlady would lose the deal.

She'd known the house was up for sale, but so far had no luck in finding somewhere else to live. As a renter, she had rights and didn't have to be out in the stipulated week, but she also knew that Marla, her landlady, had just been diagnosed with cancer and only had a limited health insurance policy. She was going to need every penny from the sale of the house to help offset her medical expenses.

For Marla, she'd move, but how was she going to find another house as convenient to her work in five days?

On top of that, there was the supposed "marriage" she found herself in, and Dillon Stone to deal with. Every time she'd tried to find sleep last night, all she'd seen were serious, dark green eyes watching her, assessing her and finding her lacking. He didn't really want her for his wife. She knew that. Their marriage was a mistake.

Then why did the faint memory of his aftershave linger in her dreams? And why did she keep thinking of his very masculine physique, strong hands and too-tempting lips, as if he really was her husband?

"Can I get you something to drink?" Dillon's polite inquiry brought Eleanor abruptly back to where she was—sitting on her so-called husband's over-stuffed khaki-colored couch in his tall-ceilinged, bright, airy living room. Late morning sunlight streamed softly through tall windows hung with dark green blinds.

"Uh...yes. Water would be fine." Anything to get Dillon's tall, distracting magnetism away from her. When he turned and left the room, Eleanor ignored the realization that she was staring at the man's back-side as if she'd never seen anything that sexy before. Well…actually, she hadn't.

"Do you know how to make chocolate-chip cook-ies?"

Eleanor glanced at Ryan, who had taken up resi-dence right next to her on the couch. He was leaning like the Tower of Pisa against her shoulder, his young eyes bright with interest and excitement.

Chocolate-chip cookies. His life was so simple. As a child, her life had never been that simple. She'd never been with one family long enough for things to be anything but complicated, but she had learned to make cookies, the only good thing besides Jake to come out of her last foster home. "Yes, I do."

"Will you help me make some today?" Ryan looked at her with such earnestness. He really wanted her to help him. The hard casing she'd erected around her heart suffered in the heat of his genuine approval. She could get used to being needed by this little guy.

Gingerly placing her arm around his slight body, she hugged him gently, allowing the comfort of hold-ing Ryan to roll over her, grasping at the feeling like a lifeline.

"I would love to make cookies with you, but I can't stay very long."

"How come?"

"Because I have to look for a new house today." Eleanor hated the disappointment she was bringing to Ryan's expressive eyes. How often as a child had she been disappointed?

"Why?"

"Because I have less than a week to find a place to live. That's not much time."

Holding a tray with one glass of water and two lemonades, Dillon stopped in the doorway, arrested by the sight of Eleanor sitting with one arm wrapped gently around his son, while Ryan leaned against her as if he'd been born to the woman. Unaware that he was there, Eleanor wore an expression that was softened with regret...and sadness, instead of masked with her usual indifference.

Something forgotten moved in Dillon's chest. There was more to Eleanor than she was willing to reveal. Maybe she wasn't the remote woman she was trying to convince him she was.

Seeing her with his son, Dillon began to wonder what, or who, had shaped Eleanor Rose...rather, Stone now...into the detached woman she worked so hard to present to the world.

"Why?" Ryan asked again.

Deciding it was time to save the poor lady, Dillon stepped into the room. Once Ryan had his sights set on something he wanted, asking *why* was his favorite way of wearing down the adult who stood between him and his objective.

"Drinks are here. What's this you were saying about having to move?" Placing the tray on the square coffee table, Dillon wasn't prepared for the unguarded look that flashed from emotionally laden brown eyes, fueling an awareness that had been building since the moment he'd first seen her enter the Harbor Room lounge.

Dillon pushed his hands into his pockets to keep from grabbing Eleanor as she stared at him as if he was the last piece of dark chocolate on the planet.

Not understanding why he suddenly wanted to be that piece of chocolate, he stepped away to stand by the fireplace.

Feeling his body's instant reaction to the need in her heated look, Dillon wondered what in the Sam Hill he was going to do now?

Then the curtain of her lush eyelashes dropped and all that riotous, storming emotion was banked… hidden as if it had never existed. Amazed, Dillon realized Eleanor was good at that—hiding her emotions.

What in the world was she doing? Eleanor blinked, mentally and emotionally stepping back from the man who was pure devastation to her senses. She was thankful she was already sitting, because even his unique smell, man mixed faintly with spicy after-shave, made her knees weak. For a moment, when their gazes locked tighter than a yin-yang symbol, it was as if he was kissing her again…tasting… exploring…claiming her as his. And, scarier still, a part of her *wanted* to be claimed by this man.

"Eleanor? You have to move?" His husky baritone wrapped her in what? Want? Need? And…?

"Oh…yeah. My landlady left me a message last night. She's decided to sell the house and has a buyer. I have to be out by the end of the week or her sale will fall through."

"You have rights. She can't just evict you like that. She has to give you notice. What she's doing isn't legal."

Eleanor was unexpectedly touched by Dillon's sudden horrified anger. When was the last time someone besides Jake had jumped so quickly to her defense?

"She's not really evicting me. It's okay. I don't mind."

"You should. As the renter, the law is very specific. It's on your side. Why are you giving up so easily? You don't strike me as the kind of woman who would do that."

What kind of woman did he think she was?

"My landlady needs the money. She has a serious medical problem," Eleanor finally said, perching on the edge of the couch. She refused to discuss Marla's private business, even to improve this man's opinion of her. "Anyway, it means I have to house hunt today."

"But you're going to live with us." At the insistence in Ryan's voice, the absurdity of her situation hit Eleanor.

All of her life she'd secretly dreamed of being part of a real family, having people close to her, who would love her without question or reservation. By the time she was nineteen, Dillon Stone had made the top of the list—actually was the only one on the list—of the perfect men to play the part of husband and father to that family.

Now, by some odd quirk of the universe, Eleanor found herself part of the family she'd always dreamed of, including that sexy husband and beautiful child. But it was all fake. She wasn't *really* a wife, nor had she given birth to Dillon's son.

"Ryan, your dad and I, we're not really—" The shrill ring of the telephone interrupted Eleanor.

Hiding a sigh of resignation, she hungrily watched Dillon as he reached for the annoying machine. Dark brown hair touched with red highlights curled haphazardly onto his strong forehead. It was cut short in the back, barely touching the collar of his shirt.

Greedy, she studied his rugged features. At thirty-four, his face had filled out, maturing with age like fine wine. Laughter lines spread from the corner of his eyes and tempting mouth. Now that mouth thinned in concentration as he listened, one hand holding the phone to his ear, the other pushed deeply into his pants pocket.

There was something very important about Dillon Stone and the love he shared with his son...and had with Joan. Something that made Eleanor suddenly feel as if she hadn't quite built the perfect life. She'd never been able to capture that illusive emotion herself, not with anybody. Had she missed something vitally important?

No. She'd made a good life without the trouble and heartbreak love brought with it. Just as it had for Dillon when his wife had died so suddenly. She'd been horrified when Jake had first told her Joan had been killed in a car accident.

No one could believe it, least of all Dillon, she remembered Jake telling her. But there was nothing anyone could do. Joan was gone, leaving Dillon all alone to raise their son.

Eleanor listened unashamedly as he talked to the person on the phone, his dark, heavy brows pulling together in a frown. Closing his stunning green eyes off from her view, he tiredly pinched the bridge of his straight nose.

"Okay, Mrs. Holloway. I hope you feel better soon." Despite her best intentions, the deep concern lacing his words wrapped around Eleanor like a fa-

vorite blanket, warming her with shivers of capti-
vation.

You have to stop this, she warned herself angrily,
trying to shake free of the spell that was weaving
itself tightly around her heart. It was an almost impossible task, since the broad shoulders stretching his
western shirt tight, his well-shaped backside encased
snugly in faded jeans, long muscular legs and bare
feet invaded her entire field of vision.

Feet? What could it be about the man's bare feet
that she found so...confusingly provocative? They
were just your average set of feet, after all. Maybe it
wasn't his feet. Maybe it was the fierce way he loved
his son that caused her aberrant heart to race? Or the
way he'd leaped to her defense when he'd heard she
needed to move so quickly? Whatever it was, she
wasn't going to find out. These sidewinder feelings
were only bad-girl hormones. Easily squashed and dis-
posed of.

Unfortunately, the sidewinders were not so easily
evaded when Dillon hung up the phone and locked
gazes with her as if he was searching for something
deep inside her soul. Eleanor couldn't stop the ricocheting shivers that started at her toes, not stopping
until they collided with her heart.

''What?'' she asked him shakily, suddenly realizing she was hanging too tightly on to Ryan's small
hand.

Dillon had felt Eleanor's silent regard, the skin on
his neck muscles twitching in blatant awareness.
When he'd turned and plunged right into pools of
wistful, dark-whiskey eyes, he'd suddenly wondered
what it would be like to hold the she-cat so close he

would feel the bite of her claws when he sought permission to take liberties with her tempting body.

For the first time, she didn't rebuke him with her defenses. Why? She was such a strange assortment of contradictions. He didn't know what to make of her. She certainly wasn't what he expected in a wife.

But she was gentle with his son. Not everyone knew how to relate to a six-year-old, he begrudgingly admitted, baffled that he even wanted to figure out the puzzle that was Eleanor Rose.

"Bad news?" The husky timbre of her voice rubbed his senses as the faint fragrance of vanilla tightened the fit of his jeans...only irritating him more.

"Yes. Mrs. Holloway has the flu. She was going to watch Ryan for me while I went to a meeting at the dean's house this evening." Breaking his thoughts away from an imaginary, but very passionate lip lock with the woman frowning at him, Dillon mentally shook himself.

Cut it out. Despite the strange circumstances, she's not the woman for you.

"I've got to think about this." *And, stop thinking about Eleanor...Stone.* "I don't know anyone else who can stay with Ryan. This meeting's important. It's my first with the other university staff members." Dillon forced himself to concentrate on this new problem. He was a lawyer, for heaven's sake. He wasn't supposed to rattle so easily.

"Miss Eleanor can stay with me!" Ryan leaped up from where he was still sitting beside Eleanor, jumping up and down in his enthusiasm.

Dillon looked at Eleanor's still face, her wide eyes watching his son's exuberance. Like a deer caught in headlights, she looked...stuck...and scared out of her wits. Her lips moved, but for a moment, the only sound that came out was a breathy squeak. Then it was as if she couldn't get words out fast enough.

"I don't think that's a good idea. You don't know me that well. And I really need to look for a place to live today."

"Please?" Ryan begged.

Dillon knew he should be a gentleman and come to Eleanor's rescue. But, he wasn't going to. Her sudden backpedaling intrigued him. Besides, he really didn't know anyone else he'd trust with Ryan. Though why he was so sure he could trust this lady, he didn't even try to understand.

"Dad?"

Dillon smiled reassuringly at his son before turning back to the woman in full-blown panic.

"My meeting's not until six. We can go house hunting between now and then. The Sunday paper came this morning, so we can get started now, if you want." Dillon frowned at his impulsive gesture. He shouldn't allow himself to be influenced by Ryan's begging eyes or Eleanor's barely hidden vulnerability.

What other person in his acquaintance, besides his sister, Beth, would move on a moment's notice because their landlord needed to sell their house for the reason Eleanor's did? That the lady was so willing to do so said something to Dillon about her that was not easily detectable or ignored once discovered. Something she was trying desperately to keep hidden. Something that was starting to make him very irritatingly curious.

Eleanor was a softhearted sap. And, Dillon had to

grudgingly admit, he liked that about her. It also meant he could use that soft heart to his advantage and convince her to stay with Ryan for the evening. Anyway, it was only for one night. He should feel bad about using her compassion against her, but he didn't. Besides, if it wasn't for her, he could be going about the business of finding himself the kind of wife he really needed.

"Well, I don't know..." Why was she thinking, even for a second, of taking part in Dillon and Ryan's life? Why couldn't she leave well enough alone? She should get the heck out of Dodge before she did something stupid like believing in the magic that was trying to weave it's spell around her. Eleanor Silks Rose...er Stone, beloved wife and mother? Yeah. Right.

"Please, Miss Eleanor?" Ryan's stubborn refusal to give up was the last straw. Eleanor looked desperately at Dillon, finding no help there. What was a woman trying to keep her heart safe supposed to do?

"Okay. Fine. I'll watch you tonight. But you, little man—" Eleanor gently poked Ryan in his tummy "—will have to help me find a new place to live this afternoon."

When a mutinous look started clouding his face, Eleanor gently poked him again, "Deal?"

Ryan was only six years old. It was ridiculous to believe he really wanted her to live with him and his dad.

You have a nice safe life. Don't go there Eleanor...Stone.

"Deal," the little boy finally agreed, looking

down at his feet and kicking unhappily at the edge of a colorful throw rug.

"Let's find that paper and get started."

At Dillon's brisk tone of voice, Eleanor glanced up at him and instantly got trapped by the frustration spearing her from his fierce look.

Surely he didn't blame her for their stupid predicament. Her heart beating madly, Eleanor wondered how she was going to survive a whole afternoon with the tormenting man. It was ludicrous to even try.

Suddenly afraid of the feelings stalking her, Eleanor felt as if she were unexpectedly emerging from a dark closet into a brightly lit room. Longing she'd thought she'd conquered long ago was growing with every passing moment she spent with Dillon and Ryan Stone.

She did not want to admire Dillon Stone.

She did not know how to be Ryan's new mom.

Chapter Five

Five hours later, Eleanor sat in the kitchen, elbow deep in flour with a very industrious little boy. White dusted his nose and his dark hair poked up in matted spikes where he'd pushed it back when it fell forward into his eyes.

Eleanor worked hard to hide a smile. As much as she hadn't wanted to, she'd enjoyed the afternoon house hunting with Dillon and Ryan. For the first time in forever, she'd been unable to resist opening the door to her fortress. Or, think about what it would be like if she and Dillon were really married. Thinking about what it would be like if she was really Ryan's new mom.

Battering her defenses, Dillon had opened doors for her. Ryan had grabbed her hand each time they got out of the truck and skipped along beside her as if he'd been doing that all his young life. She'd had a good time. And they hadn't found a house for her to move into.

For a moment, she chewed her lower lip, wondering what she was going to do. One thing was for sure. Though she could wish otherwise with all her heart, she was not really married to Dillon Stone and she was not really Ryan's mother.

The fact that neither one of her errant knights had approved of any of the houses they'd looked at didn't help. She wasn't sure at what point Dillon and his son had turned into knights in shining armor. Sometime between "This place is too small, you can't live here" and "There are rats in the basement—you can't live here, either."

And she still hadn't asked Dillon for that annulment! There hadn't been a chance with Ryan hanging on to her hand every minute.

"You guys look like you're having fun." Dillon's sudden appearance startled Eleanor from her thoughts.

Dressed in blue jeans and a sports jacket, his feet hidden in black cowboy boots, Dillon stole Eleanor's breath away. Stubbornly, she willed her erratic heartbeat to slow down and the sudden tension attacking her to go away.

"Uh...yes. Ryan was anxious to get started."

"Dad, look. I'm making chocolate-chip cookies."

Eleanor licked dry lips as she watched Dillon walk toward his son, picking up a tea towel on the way.

"I can see that," he said straight-faced, a secret smile lighting his dark green eyes. Using the towel, he swiped the flour dust from his son's hair.

"W-we'll clean up the mess when we're done," Eleanor stammered, pushing her glasses back up her nose, unable to take her eyes off the hard cowboy physique that refused to quit taunting her. Some knight in shining armor he turned out to be. He was supposed to protect her, not tempt her into the wickedest deed she could think of doing.

"I'm not sure how long this meeting will go. I might be home late."

Home. But not her home.

"That's okay. I'll make sure Ryan gets to bed." She was just the baby-sitter, not the boy's mother. How could she have given in to the temptation of pretending she was a part of their family?

"Ryan. You mind Miss Eleanor and go to bed when she says."

At the brief knuckle rub his dad gave him, Ryan looked up from the flour fortress he was meticulously building. "I will, Dad."

Dillon casually stepped around the counter, stopping right in front of her, instantly arousing all Eleanor's fragile defenses.

"Thanks. I can't tell you how much I appreciate this."

Unable to get past the man's kissable lips, Eleanor barely had enough thought left to respond. "No problem."

Then, before she knew what he was doing, Dillon gently pushed a loose strand of hair behind her ear. Eleanor's breath hitched. His touch brought the house down around her ears. The crowd roared. Electric excitement shot down to her toes. By the time she'd recovered, the man was gone...like smoke into thin air, but leaving behind a slow burn that refused to be put out.

In a daze, Eleanor helped Ryan finish the cookies...made sure he ate his dinner...explored his room with him...gave him his bath...overcame his reluctance to go to bed, and read the bedtime story the little guy insisted he must have. By the time she was done, she was exhausted from trying to keep up with one little boy and from doing everything she could to ignore the gentle curiosity that marked Dillon's touch.

Generally, she avoided anything connected with the ritual of mating. She didn't do relationships well. She was much better at her job as a corporate librarian at Smithtowers, Inc., where her responsibilities centered around providing information and data management. She had no skills to help her with this mistaken marriage or caresses that made her feel too vulnerable.

What was worse, she liked Dillon's touch. It had to be hot, sultry lust that was attacking her, trapping her. Because she'd gotten over her crush for the man a long time ago.

With Ryan safely tucked in, Eleanor hurried past the darkened room that could only be Dillon's and down the stairs, desperate to wipe a new vision of her and Dillon...together in the big bed she'd glimpsed from her fertile imagination.

When she finished cleaning the kitchen, she ignored the room that was obviously his home office, and went straight to the living room, liking the warm, masculine feel of it. No feminine touches here.

Unable to curb her curiosity, Eleanor studied the pictures there, touching each one with her fingertips, as if absorbing their energy would infuse her own life with a warmth she hadn't realized until this moment was missing.

As she looked at the pictures, one of Dillon and Ryan taken recently, another of Dillon with an older

man and a female version of himself, obviously his
dad and his sister, Eleanor realized how alone she
really was and fought the desolate feelings that insight kindled.

Taking the photograph of Dillon and Ryan with
her, she sat on the couch, studying it closely. She
traced the man's rugged features with her pinkie, noting the similarities between the devastating father
and son.

She was so tired.

Hugging the picture close to her heart, she sighed
softly, sliding lengthwise on Dillon's comfortable
couch. There was no point in wishing for the moon.
It wouldn't change things. It wasn't going to take
long for Dillon to unravel the tangle he found himself
in. Only, just this once, Eleanor really wished she
could have the moon, instead of an annulment. Just
this once…she wished…

Dillon got home later than he'd expected. He wondered if Eleanor thought he'd taken advantage of her
because he'd pushed her into baby-sitting for him. In
the kitchen earlier, she'd looked like she was having
fun, and at the same time she'd looked vulnerable,
so wistful—flour up to her elbows, dusting her chin,
and her glasses perched precariously on her nose.
Was that why he'd touched her like that? Because
she'd been just as enthusiastic about making cookies
as Ryan?

Quietly, he let himself into the dark house, noting
the light shining from the living room. Softly, he
called her name. When there was no answer, he tip-
toed into the room and found Goldilocks sleeping on

his couch. A picture was clutched loosely to her softly rising chest.

In repose, her features were serene, as if she hadn't a care in the world. Her lustrous blond hair loose and flowing over the armrest like a living stream of sunlight caused his stomach to clench like a tight fist.

The camp shirt she wore with her jeans had pulled loose, the top button freed, exposing a rounded swell of creamy, soft skin that yanked his attraction for the woman into overdrive. His instant response to the bewitching sight was becoming too familiar. How could a woman so unlike his idea of the ideal wife grab his attention so forcefully?

Squatting beside her, Dillon gently pulled a strand of her sunlight hair, smooth as one of his silk ties, back from where it had fallen across one eye. He fingered it, fascinated as it flowed from his fingertips to join the rest of her cascading mane.

She was so different from Joan and not what he wanted in a wife at all. But the fact remained, they were married. Why hadn't he talked to her about it? They needed to make some decisions. Now, with Ryan's feelings involved, those decisions were not going to be easy ones.

Standing, Dillon carefully lifted her leg from where it draped over the edge of the couch. It was too late to wake her. She slept so sweetly, more peaceful in her slumber than when she was awake and on guard.

Making a valiant effort to ignore the slight weight of her slender leg in his hands, Dillon held his breath until she rolled into the couch undisturbed, turning so her rounded derriere mocked him. A small wiggling motion to get comfortable caused a response in a part of his anatomy he was glad she wasn't awake to see.

What was wrong with him? This was the wrong time...the wrong place...and the wrong woman for that.

Pulling a blanket from the armchair, he very deliberately covered up those delectable curves. Removing the picture from her loosened grip, he recognized the photograph as one taken at Beth's wedding, just before she'd left on her honeymoon. Her last whispered words still rang in his ears.

"Now it's your turn to find love, brother. Good luck. You deserve it."

Love. He wasn't looking for love. And luck had nothing to do with finding a wife. Tired, Dillon decided he would talk to Sleeping Beauty tomorrow. Tomorrow was soon enough to clear up their confusing marriage.

When he woke the next morning, Dillon was surprised he'd slept without dreaming. His last thought before drifting off had been of Eleanor and the surprising facets of her personality he was uncovering. He couldn't picture the Eleanor he knew allowing herself to be talked into watching a little boy and then falling asleep on the couch while she waited for the father to get home.

Glancing at the clock on his nightstand, Dillon quickly got up. He'd slept in, and it was Ryan's first day of school. In a rush, he started down to the kitchen double time before realizing he wore only his boxers. They were no more than his usual sleep attire, but what he didn't normally find in his house each morning was a woman. And not just any woman.

Eleanor Rose…Stone. They needed to discuss their current marital status. That was better done fully clothed. Going back to his room and quickly pulling on an old pair of gray sweats, Dillon thought about what he wanted to say and how he wanted to say it.

Under any other circumstances, Eleanor would be the last lady on earth he'd ask to marry him, but he really didn't want to put it like that to her. They were already married and Ryan really seemed to like her. Just because she was beautiful and sexy when she forgot to stay behind her defenses… Their current situation clearly deserved further consideration.

"Hey, son, what are you doing down here by yourself?" Dillon frowned at Ryan, who sat at the table smacking down cereal, milk dripping from his chin. Grabbing a tea towel, Dillon wiped the white rivulet from his son's face. Normally, the little guy woke him up before he came downstairs in the morning.

"Miss Eleanor helped me fix my cereal," Ryan said, stuffing another spoonful in his mouth.

"Where is Miss Eleanor?" Dillon didn't like the anticipation flooding his stomach.

"She left when the little hand was on seven. She told me to give you this note." Ryan held out a folded piece of paper smudged with soggy fingerprints.

Slowly taking the limp paper, Dillon silently growled at the disappointment he refused to acknowledge. "Where'd she go?"

"To work."

"Hmm." Just his luck. The one time he needed

his son's usual chitter-chatter, the kid had to clam up on him. Dillon carefully opened the milk-logged note.

Dillon,
Please find out about an annulment today. I'll be at work. The number is 555-1344.

Eleanor

She wanted an annulment. A sneaky stab of disappointment quickly turned to anger.

Eleanor didn't want to be married to him. That was fine. He didn't want to be married to her, either. The sooner he got rid of her, the sooner he could go back to his lists and his own plan. Using reason and logic to find a wife, not runaway emotion, was the only way to go, anyway.

Wadding the missive into a ball, Dillon threw it into the sink. It was time to give the blasted woman just what she wanted.

Eleanor waited nervously for Dillon at the Harbor Room. Disgusted, she stopped herself just before she started biting her manicured nail. Why was she so anxious? It wasn't her fault they'd somehow gotten married. And it wasn't her fault she didn't feel up to be married…to anyone.

Dillon had sounded angry when he'd called to tell her to meet him. What had she done that was so terribly wrong? Obviously, he didn't want to be married to her any more than she wanted to be to him. Then why did she feel as if she had something to apologize for?

Eleanor had chosen a table facing the doorway so

she could watch for Dillon's arrival. At that moment, the heavy door swooshed open and the sight of her...temporary husband...tripped her heartbeat. Carefully, she placed her glass of wine on the table.

Who was she trying to kid? Just the sight of his tall, strong body did unholy things to her own susceptibility. But desire wasn't enough to make a relationship work. Her boyfriend in college, John Tremain, hadn't been interested in a real relationship despite his apparent, overabundant college-boy hormones. Dillon wouldn't be interested, either, after being married to Joan, who was, according to Jake, a perfect wife and mother.

"Hi."

Dillon stopped right in front of her, looking at her thoughtfully as if he was trying to read her mind. Well, he'd know soon enough what she thought.

"Hi. What did you find out? We didn't have to meet here. I could have come to your house." For a top-notch corporate librarian who passed on mounds of information succinctly, and who got her point across in the most straightforward manner, Eleanor couldn't believe, with one look at the devastating man, she'd become a babbling idiot.

"I didn't want to talk in front of Ryan," Dillon said, finally breaking that soul-searching eye contact as he sat in the chair opposite her.

"I see." Eleanor didn't like the familiar feeling of desertion that washed dangerously close to her heart. Straightening her spine, she reminded herself that this was what she wanted. What she knew would happen eventually, anyway.

"We're really married. I looked into Judge Banta's credentials and he is a judge with the authority to perform marriages." Dillon wasn't surprised to see the incredulity cross Eleanor's delicate features. He could hardly believe it himself. He and Eleanor were legally married. They needed to decide what to do about it. Dillon dismissed the persistent idea that they could make their unlikely marriage work—for Ryan's sake. Instead he concentrated on the stunned woman sitting opposite him.

"How soon can we get an annulment?"

Eleanor's quick question made Dillon angry. Ryan had really taken to her and all she could think about was how fast she could be rid of them.

"I checked with the courthouse. After we submit the petition and the affidavit for annulment, the final judgment is signed by the judge. Then it takes thirty days to become final." Dillon buried his anger. He was not going to show this woman that her need to get out of their marriage bothered him in any way. Which, of course, it didn't.

"Thirty days. I suppose ours will be the shortest marriage on record."

Surprised by the regret lacing Eleanor's husky voice as she pointedly studied the high polish on her perfectly manicured nails, Dillon was completely confused. Did the baffling woman want in or out of their wackier-by-the-moment marriage?

"How soon can you file the papers?" Eleanor's voice lost its conflicting emotions and it was back to business, her expression carefully blank, whiskey eyes locked determinedly to his. But irresistibly, hidden deep where it was almost unrecognizable…

I need a drink. "I'll be right back," Dillon said instead, then belatedly asked, "Do you want another of whatever that is you're having?'' He'd noticed she been nursing a glass of wine when he came in.

''Uh, yes. White Zin, please.''

He was being stupid, Dillon decided while he waited for the Jack Daniel's and wine he ordered at the bar. Did Eleanor want an annulment or not? He certainly did, now that he'd had a chance to think about it. Then why was he starting to feel so protective of the confounding woman? The fact that they were accidentally legally married, did not make him responsible for her.

So what if she was going to lose her house at the end of the week? So what if she was more vulnerable than she liked to let on? So what if there was a spark of uncertainty hidden deep in her expressive eyes? What did it matter that she was secretly a damsel in distress and didn't want anyone to know it?

He was not her Frog Prince and she was not his Sleeping Beauty. He liked dark-haired women, not blondes. He liked a woman who smiled a lot, not one who had to be constantly coaxed to leave behind her reserve. He was interested in a stay-at-home, mothering woman, not a corporate workaholic. The fact that he also liked whiskey-brown eyes and long, gangly legs couldn't be allowed to influence his decision about how to get out of the fix he was in.

Still undecided, he took the drinks back to the table where Eleanor was biting her fingernail.

''Why don't you move in with me?'' The shocked look on Eleanor's face was nothing compared to the appalled waves rippling through Dillon at his unfortunate choice of words.

When fear, clearly mixed with skepticism, replaced her shock, Dillon knew there was no way he could take back his offer. What had made him say those exact words he didn't know, but now *he* was the deer stuck in headlights and scared out of his wits.

"I don't know."

She was giving him a way out. He should take it.

"Look. You have to be out of your house by the weekend. It'll take at least a month to get the annulment. In the meantime, I have plenty of room at my place. Ryan will want you to stay with us." It was foolish to mention his son. Now she would never say no.

Eleanor couldn't believe what she was hearing. Dillon—her fantasy man—was asking her to move into his place. Never mind that it was only temporary, or that they were, unbelievably, legally married. Or that he was offering her a chance to be part of his most intimate family. Or that for a very short time she could be Ryan's mother. Or that for a moment in the whole cosmic scheme of things she would be Dillon Stone's almost real wife.

She couldn't move in with Dillon. What would Ryan think? Even if she did, she would only be Dillon's temporary wife. Was that what she wanted?

"I don't think that's a good idea," she said, trying one last time to fight Dillon's beguiling proposition.

"Why not? You need a place to live, and as your husband, it's my obligation to take care of you."

Eleanor felt the heat of humiliation warm her cheeks. She knew he didn't love her...but an obligation?

"I've been taking care of myself for a long time. I won't be anyone's obligation," she said angrily, pushing away a sharp stab of hurt. She'd been right all along. Why was she doing this to herself?

"Don't go ballistic. You know what I mean. You have no where else to go. And I can help."

Eleanor's anger banked as fast as it flared. She studied the mulish expression crossing Dillon's rugged features and wondered at the tug on her heart.

"What will you tell Ryan?" she asked quietly, not wanting to do a single thing that would hurt the little guy.

"The truth. That you're just moving in for a little while."

"All right. I'll move in, but only until the annulment's final." Somewhere deep inside, in a place she avoided exploring at all costs, she secretly wished she really could stay Mrs. Dillon Stone forever. It was an idea that was too scary to be examined closely.

Dillon stood in the middle of Eleanor's living room, holding the last box to be loaded into his truck. He hadn't meant to ask her to move in with him, but once the words were out, he'd done what he could to get the deed done.

He'd made the arrangements to rent a storage unit for her things, then cleared out a room down the hall from his own. With Ryan between them, it should be safe.

He'd even talked to Ryan and clearly explained the situation. Eleanor was moving in temporarily because she needed a place to stay. She was not his wife. She would have her own room. He would have his. And what he hadn't said was a sharp reminder for himself—they would not be sleeping together.

That was a little too much information for a six year old.

Sleep together. That was a laugh. Even though Eleanor had agreed to move in until the annulment was finalized or until she found a place of her own—whichever came first—she'd made it abundantly clear she didn't want to have anything to do with him. In fact, one of the few times he'd seen or heard from the woman since he'd opened his big mouth was this morning when she'd called to tell him she was all packed and ready to move.

That was fine by him. The less she interrupted his life the better. Then, once this whole sorry situation was behind him, he could get back to the serious business of finding himself the comfortable wife he wanted. A woman who would want to spend time with him and Ryan, and who would be interested in him…in them.

''Okay. I guess this is the last of it.''

Standing by the front door, Dillon watched Eleanor emerge from the back of the house shouldering a travel bag and her laptop computer. What was it about her that jump-started his libido every time he looked at her?

Today, she was wearing jeans and a tank top that molded to her slender body like a perfect glove. Her long hair was pulled back in a ponytail, making her look more like the tomboy he remembered than the twenty-eight-year-old businesswoman she'd become.

Taking a deep breath, Dillon lowered the box he was holding to hide his depraved body's reaction to the fantasy of those long legs wrapped around him while he pulled her as close as was physically possible.

"Let's go home, then," he said gruffly.

Home. Eleanor's heart lurched. Did Dillon really believe they were making a home together? In the week since she'd agreed to move in with him, she'd made herself keep her distance. Except for the brief time she'd spent in this bungalow, she'd never had a real home before. He couldn't know that he was offering her a small slice of heaven.

Eleanor followed Dillon out to his truck, placing the last of her personal belongings in the extended cab, then climbed in and fastened her seat belt. Frowning, she reminded herself that while the little scenario she was playing out—going home with Dillon Stone as his bride—might be a wild dream come true, it was also her worst nightmare. She didn't need the added complication of messy feelings in her life.

"What do you want to do about dinner?" the man beside her asked.

Holding tightly to her resolution to keep her distance, Eleanor wasn't about to tell Dillon what...or who she really wanted for dinner.

"Takeout?"

"Do you like pizza?" His question was absentminded, as he concentrated on pulling out into traffic.

"Sure." Among other things.

"Pizza it is, then."

Great, Eleanor decided, trying and failing to avoid sarcasm.

An hour later, she sat at Dillon's kitchen table eating mushroom pizza, a long string of cheese dangling between the bite in her mouth and the slice she was pulling away from her face.

The setting sun splashed through the open back door and the fragrance of fall lulled her. She'd already put her things in her "new" room, and now, across the table from her, Dillon and Ryan bantered cheerfully back and forth. For the first time in longer than she could remember, Eleanor felt tempted to open her defenses a crack and allow her new family in.

"What do you think, Miss Eleanor?"

"What do I think about what?" Eleanor looked at Ryan, who was jumping up to reach for another piece of pizza.

"Can we go to the zoo tomorrow?" he asked, poking the pointed end of the slice into his mouth.

"Can we…? Well, I was planning to get settled in and maybe get some work done."

"Please? I really want to show you the polar bears."

She won't go, Dillon wagered with himself. As much as she'd managed to shed most of her usual reserve while they ate, he'd bet his Ford pickup she wouldn't go to the zoo with them.

Her rare laughter at Ryan's pleading look took Dillon by surprise. Deep and throaty, the sound stampeded like a runaway herd down his spine, reminding him what it was like to play to the crowd of that one special woman. Eleanor was not his special woman, of course. She was a woman devoted to her career. Bringing work home only proved it. She would not go to the zoo with them.

"I've never been to a zoo."

Dillon couldn't believe what he was hearing. Every child goes to the zoo at least once in their young lives, don't they?

"You should go with us, then," he told her softly,

trying not to drown in the turbulent whiskey eyes she turned on him.

"Are you sure? I won't be intruding?"

"No, of course not."

"How come you've never been to the zoo?" Ryan had gotten down from his chair and moved to stand next to Eleanor, his small hand touching her arm in the kind of sympathy only a child could give.

Eleanor looked confused, as if she didn't understand why she'd never been to a zoo, either. "I never had anyone who wanted to take me."

Dillon's gut tightened painfully as the proud woman straightened her shoulders, feverishly blinking her expressive eyes to prevent the fall of sudden, welling tears. He knew Eleanor had been raised in foster homes, but he couldn't believe there had been no one to take the lonely child she must have been on such an outing. Anger snaked though his heart at the neglect.

"You should go with us," his son whispered, repeating Dillon's own invitation.

"I'd really like to go with you," Eleanor whispered back through a shaky smile, flicking her gaze to his, as if she was sure he would take his invitation back and not let her go.

Dillon traced the shy smile lighting her aloof, beautiful features as she let Ryan put his arms around her and hang on tight. Slowly, her arms found their way around his son's slight body, returning the child's hug with a hesitant, tight squeeze.

There was definitely more to Eleanor Rose Stone than she wanted to reveal. Maybe, it was time he found out more about the lady, who without any effort on his part and against his best intentions, was now his legal wife.

Chapter Six

Eleanor woke the next morning to find Ryan standing at her bedside watching her.

"What are you doing, little man?" She eyed him sleepily, stretching her arms over her head to loosen up sleepy kinks.

"I'm waiting for you to wake up. Dad said—"

"Ryan. Where are you?" Dillon's whispered voice was followed by his handsome face, peering around the corner of her door into her bedroom just as she finished stretching.

Dark eyes slowly raked her from fingertips to toes as Eleanor realized the bedcovers had slipped, leaving a good portion of her uncovered to her waist. Thank goodness she had a nightshirt on. It was old and tatty, but at least it hid her unexpected reaction to that slow, hungry perusal and the sight of the man's shockingly bare torso.

Slowly, so as not to give away her embarrassing

aroused response, Eleanor casually pulled the covers up to her chin.

"Do you guys always wake a girl up this way?" Her breath caught at the knowing glint that sparkled in Dillon's eyes.

"Not always, but today is special. It's not every day the Stone boys get to take a pretty lady on her first trip to the zoo."

Eleanor couldn't stop the crop of goose bumps that erupted at the lazy teasing in Dillon's deep voice. What had gotten into him? Surely the man wasn't flirting with her? Quickly, she grabbed her glasses from the bedside table and jammed them onto her face.

Careful, Eleanor Rose, you're in way over your head.

"Well, the sooner you guys get out of here, the sooner I can get up and get dressed." Eleanor was sorry she sounded so gruff, but embarrassment ruled.

Grinning, the irritating man stunned her with one last, lingering appraisal before he leisurely turned to leave her room, pulling a smiling little boy out with him.

When Eleanor could no longer see Dillon's sexy backside, she energetically fanned the heat flushing her skin. She had to stop seeing this man as responsible, kind, handsome, charming...and as sexy as hell.

You're already married to this stud muffin, a small, forbidden voice whispered in her too-ready-to-listen ear.

How many times did she have to remind herself how badly this was going to turn out if she ever abandoned her rules and allowed herself to believe in the possibility of love?

She had to protect herself at all costs. And that's exactly what she intended to do. Starting right now, she decided, forcefully wiping the image of a highly amused Dillon Stone from her fertile imagination.

Dillon covertly watched the woman who occupied more and more of his thoughts as she looked at the reptiles with his son. They'd gotten to Washington Park Zoo about eleven o'clock, and now, four hours later, they'd managed to explore every square inch of the grounds and exhibits. He and Ryan always left the best for last—the polar bears. That was their next stop.

Content to be just an interested bystander, Dillon enjoyed the changes he was seeing in his son. More surprising was the sight of Eleanor, the bastion of corporate personhood with her corporate mask no-where in sight.

And she wasn't wearing her glasses. Dillon was intrigued.

Unfortunately, he couldn't stop wondering what it would be like to wrap his arms around this laughing Eleanor, the first-time zoo-goer…or to kiss her fin-gertips and leisurely make his way up to her full, smiling mouth. What would it be like to put passion in those dark, smoldering eyes…to heat her up past boiling?

He had to stop thinking about Eleanor like that. She wasn't his type, and it had been a long time since he'd allowed his hormones to rule his head. But at the moment, as he leaned against the wall opposite the exhibit enclosure, he couldn't seem to remember why she wasn't right for him. Feelings as hot and sultry as a southern delta night washed over him. He'd been to New Orleans once as a young man and had never forgotten the simmering sensuality of the southern nights that now reminded him so much of his new bride.

"Dad. Look, it's an alligator!"

Eleanor and Ryan were standing as close to the animal as the enclosure would allow. Eleanor's hand rested protectively on his son's shoulder, forcing Dillon to think about what Ryan had been missing, with his mom being gone. Dressed in jeans and a T-shirt with frolicking wolf cubs stamped on the front, the woman today was a far cry from the corporate image she presented the rest of the time.

Who was this mysterious woman who seemed to care about his son and at the same time had the power to make his body wonder what it would be like to forget its celibate state? What he needed was a loving, caring mother for Ryan, not a hot, sultry sexpot for himself.

"Stop smearing the glass with your noses, you two." Dillon moved to join them, laughing at their eagerness until he caught their combined reflections in the glass enclosure. Eleanor stood on one side of his son, he on the other. Sh...oot. What had he done, inviting this woman into their lives?

"This is so cool," Ryan said, his face pressed close to the glass separating them from the reptiles.

A large group of preschoolers, each holding another's hand, crowded around them, oohing at the sight of the lazily sleeping reptile.

"It's very cool, son. Let's move back so these

other kids can see, too.'' Taking Ryan's hand, Dillon stepped back to let the kids closer to the enclosure.

Glancing at Eleanor, he saw that they had Ryan safely between them, and that she was starting to move back as well, a look of nervousness replacing her earlier enjoyment. Suddenly, she cried out, stumbling as she tried desperately to keep her balance.

Not fast enough to keep her from falling, Dillon watched horrified as she twisted to keep from crushing the children packed close to her, a look of pain splashing across her face. A soft whoosh of air escaped her as she landed hard on the cement floor.

Like dominoes, Eleanor's hard impact unbalanced Ryan, who still held tightly to her hand, landing the little boy on top of her chest. In the next instant, Dillon heard a child scream, ''It's a monster,'' and chaos erupted around his legs.

Small, pinching hands grabbed him and a wiggling body pushed its way between his legs. Caught by surprise, Dillon lost his footing and landed with a grunt on top of Eleanor and Ryan.

''Dad. Get off of me,'' Ryan croaked.

Eleanor struggled to catch her breath. Doused in sudden pain and feeling the pressure of the man's knee on her thigh, she gasped as she moved her foot protectively, then made a desperate effort to suck needed air into pained lungs.

Then Dillon moved, placing his knee firmly between her legs, too close to… She couldn't possibly be thinking of that at a time like this…could she? A little oxygen-deprived, Eleanor shifted uncomfortably as slow, melting warmth began low in her belly and spread up through her chest. She'd just toppled Dillon and Ryan off their feet, embarrassing the h…eck out of herself and all she could do was en-vision playtime with the man doing his best to get off her.

"Eleanor, are you okay? Ryan move back…. El, look at me. Breathe."

Dillon's deep concern rolled over Eleanor, igniting flames of tingling surprise, the demand in his com-manding voice impossible to ignore. Drawing in a resistant breath, she finally forced more air into her lungs, shuddering with the effort.

"God, El. Answer me," Dillon demanded.

Did he call me El? Only Jake calls me El. Rocked by the hint of fear in his voice, Eleanor made herself respond.

"I'm okay, I think. Just embarrassed. My an-kle…" She savagely ground her teeth as someone bumped her foot.

"Stand back, kids. Give us some room,"

Eleanor could imagine Dillon's courtroom pres-ence as he started to take control. When he went as far as to put his arm around her to help her stand, Eleanor carefully pushed him back.

"I think I can do this," she told him faintly, not wanting to have anyone, especially the man who hap-pened, for now, to be her husband, so up close and personal. "Where's Ryan? Is he okay?"

When the child stepped from behind his dad, the sight of his eyes round with worry pinched Eleanor's heart. Reaching out to the little guy, she smiled ten-tatively, snagging a small grin in return.

"Ryan, can you help me up? I tripped on some-thing that rolled. What in the world was it?"

"This," Dillon said, picking up a baby bottle and holding it up for her inspection.

Ignoring her discomfort, Eleanor gingerly stood, only to be rewarded by a sharp pain shooting up from her injured ankle.

"Aah…" She made it up on one leg, favoring the other as she leaned gratefully against Dillon, who'd instantly moved to stand protectively behind her.

"What's wrong?"

"My ankle. I must have sprained it." A single tear attempted to escape from her tightly shut eyes. She never cried. Not when she'd learned she'd been abandoned at the hospital just after she was born. Not when she'd had to leave foster home after foster home when she was a kid, knowing no one loved her enough to keep her. And not when her crush for the man of her dreams had ended when he'd married another woman. She definitely wasn't going to cry now.

Without a word, strong arms lifted her, carrying her away from the crowd. Shaken and sinfully weak, Eleanor laid her head on Dillon's shoulder, indulging in the safety his arms offered, while trying to ignore the ankle that was beginning to throb with a dull jungle beat.

"Someone call the first-aid station," Dillon said to the young couple hurrying toward him.

Heart pounding, he gently placed Eleanor on a bench against the far wall. For a tall woman she was as light as a feather. She looked so pale with her eyes closed like that. Carefully, he ran his hands lightly down her leg to her injured ankle. At her sudden gasp, he looked up to see her clench her jaw in tight control.

"Sorry. Can you move your foot at all?"

At that moment a young woman dressed in black

slacks and a white lab coat pushed her way through the crowd surrounding them. "Let me through, folks." A stethoscope hung around her neck and she carried a first-aid bag.

"Hi. I'm Julie. I'm a nurse. Tell me what happened."

Eleanor sighed with relief when Dillon moved back, removing his big, probing hands from her leg. While he'd been very gentle, all she could think about was those hands exploring...and probing other parts of her body.

What was wrong with her?

"I tripped on a baby bottle." *Because I was drooling over my...husband.* She was never going to live this down. "There's a sharp pain in my ankle when I try to stand."

"Okay. Let's see what you've done." Nurse Julie was way too cheerful, she decided, gritting her teeth. What she'd done was make a fool of herself in front of Dillon Stone, the one man who could turn her world upside down. Literally and figuratively. Eleanor sucked in breath as the nurse professionally checked her ankle.

"I don't think it's broken, but it wouldn't hurt to have it checked out by an E.R. doc. Can you stand on it?"

Before Eleanor could answer, Dillon was right beside her offering to help. She hesitated only briefly before putting her hand in his, using his strength as leverage to stand.

"I don't think I need to see a doc—" Eleanor almost bit her tongue in an effort to keep the pain ricocheting through her ankle from reaching her brain.

"Man…" She plunked back to the seat. "I can't."

Ryan leaned into her shoulder, while the nurse pulled an Ace bandage out of her first-aid bag.

"We'll have to wrap this until you get to the emergency room. You'll probably need X rays."

"Are you going to die?" Ryan's round, scared eyes broke Eleanor's heart, putting her ankle in its proper perspective.

Pulling the little boy into her arms, she whispered close to his ear, "No, sweetie. I'm not going to die."

"Promise?"

"I promise." Still hugging the child, she looked up in time to witness Dillon's valiant attempt to blink away his emotions at his son's reaction. He still loves Joan, Eleanor realized, her heart contracting with a pain that left her ankle in the dust. There was no competing with the kind of love he must have had for Ryan's mother. Even if she wanted to, she couldn't do it.

"She'll need to stay off that ankle until she's seen in the E.R. I'll get a wheelchair."

"No. I'll take care of her. Ryan, can you take Miss El's bag?"

Eleanor squashed a crazy urge to giggle hysterically, torn between that and crying like a baby. She was so stupid. In the grander scheme of things, compared to Dillon's loss of Joan, a woman he'd loved enough to have a child with, it was just her ankle that was hurt, after all. Her heart had no right to feel as if it were breaking into a million, tiny irreparable pieces.

Later that night, Eleanor leaned back into the comfort of Dillon's couch, her foot propped on the coffee

table. Thanks to modern medicine, she knew her ankle was only sprained and drugs dimmed the pain to
a low throb.

Tiredly, she looked at the crutches leaning on the
couch next to her. She'd gotten them at the hospital,
which was a good thing, since she didn't want to get
used to Dillon carrying her from place to place. Being lifted in the man's arms as if she were no more
substantial than a child knocked the breath out of her.

It was just the drugs talking, but no one had ever
carried her that she could remember and she liked
the sensation of being held close to Dillon's hard
chest. Liked the feeling of his heartbeat when she
laid her head on his strong shoulder. Liked being
engulfed by the heady smell of his aftershave. Her
sense of belonging to the man came too close to her
heart's armor for comfort.

"Finally, he's asleep," the object of her imagin-
ings said, appearing in the living room doorway with
his shirttail out, and in his stocking feet. "Do you
want something to drink? Or do you want to head
straight to bed? You've had a very long day."

"Water would be great." Eleanor's earlier drows-
iness disappeared the moment Dillon's deep voice
danced over her skin like a caress. What woman in
her right mind wouldn't be attracted to Dillon Stone?
she asked herself, slightly woozy.

"Here you go." The blasted man sat right next to
her as he handed her a glass of cold water.

"Thanks."

"I'm sorry your first trip to the zoo turned out to
be so miserable." Dillon couldn't remember the last
time he'd been so shaken by a simple accident.

"That's one way of putting it. It was certainly

memorable. What could be more embarrassing than tripping over a baby bottle?''

"It can't be near as bad as the time I was bicycling through the Denver area with my sister and we passed by a lady in a tight miniskirt. I flipped head and feet over the handlebars and landed right at the woman's feet. Beth still won't let me live that one down.'' As he'd hoped, Eleanor's shoulders shook slightly, while she slumped back into the couch, her eyes dancing tiredly with amusement.

"Is that laughter I hear, Miss Rose?'' He hammed, strangely struck by the change in Eleanor as she tried unsuccessfully not to laugh at him. "Go ahead. Get it out of your system.''

"I would never laugh at you, Mr. Stone.''

But Dillon could see she was. And her suppressed amusement suddenly made him very aware.

"Well, besides tripping over a baby bottle, how did you like your first zoo experience?''

"I had a great time, thank you.''

Eleanor's voice was so drowsy and soft, Dillon had to lean close to hear her. What an ego-leveling day. He couldn't believe how independent the woman half dozing beside him was. She hadn't wanted his help at all. He should be used to it. In many ways, she reminded him of Beth, who was just as fiercely independent.

"Tell me about your sister.''

Eleanor asking about the subject of his thoughts was uncanny. Dillon shifted uneasily, fighting a strong urge to draw the woman protectively into his arms.

"Did you know we're only about ten months

apart?'' Dillon inched away, turning so he would keep his hands to himself. It was better that way.

''No.''

Unable to take his eyes from Eleanor's lips, which were moistened with the water she was sipping, Dillon cleared his throat of a sudden obstruction, jerking his gaze to the slender hand holding the glass. ''I'm the oldest. Beth's a history teacher. She got married a little over a month ago.''

''I suppose you're really close to her.'' Eleanor's voice was wistful, her eyes closed, loaning her a look of innocence that wasn't hers when she had her guard up. Despite his decision to stay away from Eleanor Rose...Stone, Dillon was intrigued by her uncharacteristic curiosity and moved an inch closer.

''Yes. How 'bout you? I know Jake is your foster brother. How about the rest of your family?'' Jake had always said that he was Eleanor's only relation. When that sense of innocence was replaced by her usual tense indifference, Dillon realized he'd stepped too close and regretted it.

Eleanor was as prickly as a cactus. It didn't take much to get all her thorny defenses up and running at peak capacity. As the silent moment stretched out, he wondered if she would answer his question.

''I don't have any other family. My mother left me at the hospital right after she filled out my birth certificate, and I don't know who my father is.''

''El. I'm sorry.'' Dillon was shocked. Sympathy washed over him. Hearing her speak of her abandonment in stark, naked words, devoid of any emotion, made him ache for the rigid woman sitting next to him. Hesitantly, he reached out to touch her shoulder, only to have his fingers tangle in the shiny cascade of her hair.

At his touch, Eleanor turned her head. "It was a long time ago. There's nothing to be sorry about. Besides, it wasn't so bad. I met Jake at my last foster home. I was thirteen and he was seventeen. He treated me like I was really his sister. A few years later, I applied for legal emancipation and got a job. No one wanted a smart-mouthed kid. So, I got out as soon as I could. No big deal."

Dillon pulled gently on the strands of hair he'd automatically wrapped around his fingers. He remembered too well the young tomboy who followed her foster brother everywhere.

Anger torched Dillon. He knew from his days as a court lawyer that there were a lot of kids, just like Eleanor, who fell through the cracks. He hadn't understood how parents could abandon their kids then. He understood it even less now.

"Jake wanted me to stay with him," Eleanor countered. "So, I did for a little while, but eventually I got out on my own. I had a plan."

Dillon saw Eleanor's small, proud smile and wasn't surprised.

"I believe it. I'll bet you've always got a plan," he told her quietly with an admiration he was startled to admit to.

She turned to look at him, her smile reaching those whiskey eyes. "You do? Well, my plan was to get an education and then get a great-paying job so that I could be totally independent. I didn't want to be obligated to anyone."

Dillon's heart went out to the girl who had given up so much in her quest for independence and stability. He suspected there was a lot more to Eleanor's story than she was saying, but he didn't press her.

Instead, he watched her stick out that stubborn chin of hers, dislodging a tendril of hair from the lock still curled around his fingers. Closing the small distance between them, Dillon carefully unwound himself from her hair, then ran his finger down the single, soft strand, beginning at her scalp and ending where the silky fibers rested on her breast. Of their own will, his knuckles skimmed over her satin skin at the point where it disappeared beneath her T-shirt.

"That must have been lonely. Have you ever thought of sharing your life with someone? A boyfriend or a husband?" At her quick look, Dillon amended, "A real husband. One of your own choosing, I mean."

Unbidden, he wondered if she dated much. Maybe there was someone special for her out there. Not that he cared one way or the other, he decided, shifting to relieve the tight fit of his jeans.

"No. I've been too busy to go looking for a husband. I'm tired. I'm going to go to bed."

So, no boyfriends or potential husbands lined up. Dillon thought of his lists. When Eleanor started to reach for her crutches, he grabbed them, moving the wooden supports out of her reach. "I'll take you up."

Dillon couldn't explain why he felt so protective of the woman scowling at him. All he could think of was the child who'd had no one to take care of her, and then after a while, in order to protect herself, wouldn't grant anyone the pleasure of getting close enough to do so.

"I can make it on my own."

"I know you can." Dillon frowned at Eleanor's determination to stand on her own two feet. A determination he had to admit he admired.

"Tomorrow you can go up and down those stairs all you want. Tonight, you're going to let me carry you." Dillon used his lawyer's voice, challenging her, earnest in his desire that just this once, she was going to let him help. Suddenly, engaged in a contest of wills, he arched his eyebrow and stared into stormy eyes, doing his best not to drown in them.

When Eleanor broke contact first, Dillon didn't give her a chance to change her mind, but simply lifted her from the couch, liking her look of irritation and the conquering-hero feeling it caused to pulse through him.

"No need to thank me," he told her, cocky at his little victory. He loosened his hold slightly, letting Eleanor drop about an inch, getting what he wanted—her arms wrapped tightly around his neck as he started up the stairs with his light burden. His hunter instincts were clearly cut loose from their moorings.

"That wasn't nice," Eleanor said into his neck, her breath warming his already sensitized skin, causing shivers to sneak down his spine.

"I know."

"Put me down." Her voice sounded husky. Could she possibly be as affected as he was by their chest-to-chest proximity?

Entering her bedroom, Dillon stopped beside the bed, releasing her legs so they dropped until just the tip of her toes were touching the rug. She was just the right height, he realized, oblivious to everything but the woman standing totally still in his arms.

"You can let me go now," she said in a hoarse whisper.

"What if I don't want to let you go just yet?" Heating up at the tremor in Eleanor's voice, Dillon wondered exactly what he did want from her.

Suddenly, it didn't matter. What mattered was Eleanor's slender body pulled snugly against his, bringing her lips tantalizingly close. Dillon watched, mesmerized as her tongue nervously moistened their lushness. Instantly reacting, he rubbed his own lips along the path her tongue had taken, unaccountably heating his blood past boiling. This couldn't be happening. This was Eleanor Rose...Stone. What was he thinking? Certainly not with his logical lawyer's mind.

When Eleanor didn't offer resistance—they were married, after all—Dillon's arousal flamed. Triggered by her hesitant acceptance, as if she wasn't sure how to proceed, Dillon gave up fighting the overwhelming attraction bombarding him, his hands burying themselves in her luscious hair. Did she know what her apparent innocence did to him—would do to any man?

Measuring her tentative response, Dillon began a slow, seductive dance, his tongue with hers, encouraging Eleanor to play in kind. She didn't disappoint him, pushing his desire to a bonfire flame. Gradually, he gave up her lips for the spot where her throat pulsed with a runaway beat, his hands roaming down her spine, bringing her firm breasts as close to his chest as he could get them.

Eleanor's eager awakening wiped all rational thought from Dillon's mind, like hitting the delete button on his keyboard. Finding the edge of her

T-shirt, he tunneled beneath the soft cotton, luxuri-
ating in the feel of the silky skin he found hidden
there. Shifting so he could trace her bra from back
to front, he could think of only one thing he wanted
at that moment. He had to hold the heavy globes his
fingers were outlining. He had to see them. He had
to taste them.

Giving Eleanor a chance to protest, Dillon slowly
pulled the confining top over her head and tossed it
on the bed. The look of unfulfilled desire that
warmed her expressive eyes almost defeated any idea
Dillon had of taking his time…of going slowly so he
didn't give her reason to change her mind. He was
certain she wanted what he wanted. The ultimate
joining of man and woman.

"You are so beautiful. What happened to the tomboy I used to know?" he asked, running his finger
slowly just inside her bra strap, then along the lacy
cup, stopping in the small tight space between her
breasts.

Chapter Seven

Dillon felt Eleanor's shivery response, saw her eyes flame with unmanageable desire and couldn't stop himself from following the path of his finger with his lips. A small lick here. A careful nip there. A full-fledged kiss to the spot between the gorgeous mounds that accepted his homage with liquid tremors.

Palming each jeans-clad cheek, Dillon pulled Eleanor into the curve of his desire, molding her supple body to his. Deciding she wasn't nearly close enough, he dove in with another mind-destroying kiss, feeling suddenly clumsy in his attempt to unsnap her jeans.

Eleanor's sudden drag of breath as his knuckles brushed her navel gave Dillon the room he was desperate for.

In a moment of utter stillness, he suddenly realized Eleanor had grasped his hands, halting his attempt to unsnap and unzip her pants. She was panting heavily, her look distracted as she leaned away from him, plopping tiredly onto the bed.

"That tomboy you knew grew up. You don't really want to do this."

"I don't?" He gulped, the remoteness of her voice splashed like cold water on his out-of-control desire.

"You don't. If we do…this, we can't get an annulment." Eleanor distractedly pushed her hair away from her face.

"An annulment." Dillon ground his teeth painfully. He hated sounding like an idiot, especially when all he could see was a scared little girl staring out of Eleanor's eyes. A scared little girl, who'd never had anyone to take care of her. Ever. And who was now vehemently pushing him away.

Get a grip! He warned himself.

"You're right." Dillon tried not to let his frustration show in his voice. He wasn't successful. He had to get out of her bedroom. Fast. The hurt look on Eleanor's face spelled disaster if he didn't plan to wrap her up in his arms and hold on tight.

"Don't worry about it, El. Just chalk it up to raging hormones," he said, carefully backing out the door. "I don't know about you, but I haven't been with anyone in a long time." With that stupid, asinine remark slipping past his lips, Dillon turned and made good his escape.

Well, hell. He should have at least pretended he was a gentleman. Heading for the shower, Dillon continued to swear softly. How was he ever going to explain to Eleanor that even though she wasn't the woman he was interested in making his lifelong mate, even though she didn't meet even one of his criteria for an acceptable, comfortable wife, he found her, to his uncomfortable dismay, incredibly attractive and sexy? And now, to make matters even worse, he couldn't keep his mind...or his hands off her.

Eleanor stared at Dillon's back as he left her room, frustrated tension radiating from his stiffly held body. Fighting tears, she couldn't blame him for being angry.

As soon as he'd lifted her in his arms to carry her up the stairs to her room, she should have stopped him. But she hadn't. She'd wanted him to kiss her, to touch her in places she'd never let any man touch her before this. His kiss, his lips on her skin, the slow exploration of his hands, whisked her reason away. Never had she wanted to consummate a kiss the way she had with the man who'd just stomped from her room.

More shaken by her encounter than she wanted to admit, Eleanor slowly stood and carefully hobbled to close the bedroom door behind him. Taking a deep breath to steady her ravished nerves, she leaned heavily against the door, closing her eyes in concentration.

Of course he wanted an annulment. He'd said it himself. He hadn't been with a woman in a long time. Feeling lingering warmth still heating her skin, Eleanor wondered how she could so recklessly let her feelings escape the closet she'd stuffed them in so long ago.

Wasn't this the laugh of the century. A twenty-eight-year-old virgin, throwing herself at the first man she'd ever had a crush on...a crush she'd thought buried nine years ago. It didn't help one bit that no other man she'd met since had measured up to the ghost of her love.

It was going to be a long night. Eleanor sighed, ruthlessly cutting off visions of Dillon being a good daddy to Ryan...of him caring that she'd had to move from her home...of his shock that she'd never been to the zoo...of him trying to take care of her when she'd stupidly hurt herself...of the sizzling passion that darkened his expressive eyes.

Sleep was definitely out of the question. Eleanor tried not to listen as the shower turned off down the hall. Picking up her T-shirt, she tossed the offending garment into a corner, making a valiant attempt to ignore the memory of soft fabric brushing her skin as Dillon had pulled it over her head.

Rapidly dressing in her tatty nightshirt and flannel bottoms, she flipped on her laptop and forced her chaotic thoughts into order. Order was what her life was made of, what made it run smoothly. Order was what she needed most now.

Sitting on the bed, her back braced against the headboard, Eleanor methodically began the search where she'd left off...obituaries within a fifty-mile radius of Portland, starting on the day of her birth. Delilah Marie Silks. The name listed on her birth certificate as her mother. She wasn't sure why she'd started with the obits. Maybe in some sick sort of way, if her mother was dead, that would explain why she'd been abandoned all those years ago.

Of course, she didn't really believe her mother was dead. It was just a place to start. She'd been left at the hospital because the woman who'd given birth to her didn't want her. Plain and simple. But Silks was an unusual name. If she could find an aunt or uncle, she might get the answers to where her mother and the rest of her family—if she had any—had been all this time.

Pushing aside a sigh of regret, the first she'd felt since that day she'd sat in a church pew watching a wedding that wasn't hers, Eleanor did what she always did—poured all her mental resources into finding the smallest detail. It made her good at her job. It would make it possible for her to find this needle in a haystack. And in the process she would forget the forbidden feelings Dillon Stone roused so easily.

Delilah Marie Silks. Where are you? Who are you? Why did you leave your baby to be raised by complete strangers? Was it something I did? Or simply that you couldn't be bothered with an unwanted kid?

Watching Dillon with Ryan, and knowing the man would walk through fire for his child, Eleanor suddenly had to know. Who was the woman her birth certificate said was her mother? And, where had she been the last twenty-eight years?

The next morning, Dillon waited impatiently for Eleanor to come down from her room. Trying to sleep had been a useless exercise and he suspected his new housemate had found it as hard to sleep as he had. The faint sound of her keyboard had irritated him clear into the early hours of the morning.

Pacing from the doorway back to his desk, where he could clearly see the stairs and Eleanor when she finally came down, Dillon picked up the papers he'd left there moments before.

Looking at the annulment papers he had ready for her to sign, he didn't understand his reluctance. He wouldn't have voluntarily chosen the tall, slender blonde for his wife. He liked small, delicate, dark-haired women. He thought about Joan and remembered how she needed his strength and protection. Eleanor didn't need or want him in any way.

Placing the legal papers back on his desk and reaching for the shelf next to his computer, Dillon pulled the book on Old West mining towns Beth had sent him. Carefully, he withdrew his lists from it's yellowed pages.

Kind.
Gentle.
Likes to cook.
Keeps a clean house.
Likes to garden.
Loves children and animals.
Happy to stay at home.
Would make a great mom for Ryan.
Would make a comfortable companion.

All characteristics that he wanted in his future wife. All characteristics that he'd admired in Joan.

He missed Joan. But she'd been gone for four years. It was time to get on with his life. And not only his own life, but Ryan's as well. He glanced at the other list.

Jane Pladget.
Theresa Wilde.
Trudy Kruiz.
Connie Blain.
Mary Towers, Bachelorette number two.

No matter how hard he stared at the piece of paper in his hand, he still couldn't find Eleanor Rose listed there.

Remembering the impossible woman's reaction to his kisses stirred Dillon. In more ways than one. He hadn't been trying to take advantage of her, but after carrying her close and witnessing just how vulnerable she could really be, he hadn't been able to stop himself from testing her need with the feel of his hands on her skin, the taste of her lips on his.

Dillon shook his head. She wasn't his ideal woman. She wasn't anything like...Joan.

Suddenly realizing what he was thinking, Dillon swore. Roughly, he ran his fingers through his hair as he sat up abruptly in his desk chair. How could he have been so stupid? What was he doing? Looking for a comfortable companion who would be a replacement for Joan? Joan had been his college sweetheart. He'd loved her with all of his heart and they'd made Ryan together. Was he really trying to get on with his life or just trying to recapture a part of his heart that he missed. Desperately.

Now he was married to Eleanor. Married to someone he wouldn't have given a thought to spending the rest of his life with. Married to a woman he was hotly attracted to. As confusing as all this made him feel, Dillon knew one thing for certain. By her response to him last night, Eleanor was just as attracted to him as he was to her, no matter how much she waved an annulment in his face.

"If we do this, we can't get an annulment."

She was right. It wouldn't work. He wanted a woman whose priority was to stay home and build a family with him. Eleanor was a career woman. He wanted someone who would be willing to share her warmth and caring with him. She wasn't.

Eleanor was independent as hell, determined to keep herself apart from the whole world...apart from him. He couldn't blame her, now that he knew how alone she'd been as a child. Frustrated, Dillon thought of the brief moments when he'd seen a softer side peek out of the barricade she'd erected around herself.

Dillon placed the lists and the annulment papers in a folder that he absently marked with Eleanor's name. Hearing a quiet brush of feet on the stairs, he quickly buried the file in his desk drawer.

"Hi." Eleanor's soft voice reached him from the doorway. Snapping the drawer shut, Dillon barely missed closing the dang thing on his fingers. He bit his lip to keep from swearing out loud.

"Hi, yourself. How's the ankle?" Dillon couldn't take his eyes off the sight of Eleanor, her hair hanging loose, flying in every direction, eyes only half open, skin still flushed with the warmth of her bed. It was not a good sign that he was inspired by her early morning look.

"Mmm." She glanced at her ankle. "Better. I didn't get to sleep until really late."

Dillon almost laughed at the look that crossed Eleanor's face the moment she really woke up and realized she was standing in his office doorway, in her pj's, talking to him as if she woke up to him every morning. Something powerful pulled in his groin at the brief pleasure that moved in her liquid eyes, before wariness replaced her sleepy contentment.

He was unreasonably irritated—and for no reason

he could explain—when her shoulders straightened and her gorgeous eyes became shielded. It hurt like h...eck. Why should he care if she stiffened and withdrew every time he came near, as if he was a toad requiring her kiss to be turned into a prince?

"Look. I'm sorry about last night. I shouldn't have said what I said."

"No big deal." Eleanor found herself fascinated by the flush of frustrated embarrassment climbing to Dillon's chiseled cheekbones.

"I was a jerk."

"Probably." Warily, she studied the red-faced man drumming his fingers on his desk. Even standing in the doorway, she was too close to protect herself from his strong personality. Images refused to stay locked away—the feel of his hands on her skin, his lips tempting her beyond reason. Unrelieved passion darkening the green of his eyes to a stormy forest color.

Eleanor frowned, beating off the unwanted reminders of just how much she'd enjoyed...and wanted Dillon's bold advances. In all honesty, she had to admit their current situation was not entirely the law professor's fault.

"Forget it. Last time I heard, it takes two to tango. I'm pretty sure you weren't all alone in last night's action," she told him uneasily. Anxious to sever the wavering connection between them, Eleanor stuck her hand out toward Dillon, who stared at her as if he couldn't believe her. "Really. No problem. Friends?"

"Friends," Dillon agreed slowly, coming from behind his desk to take her hand in his. The look in his dratted eyes disagreed with the one softly spoken word.

"How about breakfast?"

That look made her feel giddy. She was not the giddy type.

"Um. Sure."

"Do you want an omelet?"

"Who's cooking it?" Eleanor almost laughed at the abrupt, suspicious look that crossed Dillon's rugged features. Maybe this wasn't going to be so bad, after all. If she could just keep the man off his feet, so to speak, she just might save herself from being monstrously hurt by the illusion of love that was attacking her from all sides.

"You do know how to cook, don't you?" he asked weakly.

Eleanor enjoyed the sound of disbelief in Dillon's deep voice. "I thought that's what fast-food places were for."

"Figures. If I'm cooking, you're doing the clean up."

Eleanor didn't miss the sigh of long suffering behind her as she led the way to the kitchen. Not liking the swell of romantic nonsense that tried to capture her, she ruthlessly quashed the longing that washed over her. She couldn't give in to the thoughts of family and love that Dillon painted. Not if she wanted to come out of their strange marriage with her heart still in one undisturbed piece.

Friday night, Eleanor dragged herself home from work, more tired than she'd been in a long time. Unable to summon her usual concentration, she'd found her job, which she normally loved, especially tedious during the week.

Then that morning, while helping Ryan get ready for a sleepover with his new friend, Billie, Eleanor had found herself worrying endlessly about the little guy. To her, he seemed awfully young to be staying away from home. She couldn't understand why Dillon was going along with this plan—Dillon and Ryan going out for dinner, then Dillon dropping his son off at Billie's before going on to another faculty meeting.

Admonishing herself not to overreact, she tried to keep in mind Dillon had been a father a lot longer than she'd been a pseudo-mom. He knew what things were safe for Ryan to do and what things weren't safe.

Opening the freezer, Eleanor contemplated the selection of frozen dinners she'd stocked there, irritated that she wasn't as happy as she should be about getting some time alone. The week since she'd told Dillon they were just friends had been long and frustrating. She'd barely seen the man. She'd worked hard to avoid him but was not going to admit she'd missed him, which would be stupid and dangerous.

He hadn't believed her when she'd given him the news flash that she didn't cook. Irritated by Dillon's disbelief, Eleanor almost wished she could whip up a gourmet meal just to prove to him how wrong he was about her. As if she wasn't the perfect woman just because she would rather eat toadstools than cook.

Besides, she knew how to make chocolate-chip cookies. That was good enough for Ryan and certainly good enough for her.

Suddenly Eleanor smiled, remembering the comical look on Dillon's face when she'd brought home the sack of groceries filled with easy-to-prepare foods. Nothing fancy. Just food a working girl would consider essential, food that didn't have to be cooked at all or that only needed minimal help to be edible.

Finishing every bite of her microwaved lasagna and hastily made salad, Eleanor took a leisurely shower, then dressed in the new pj's she'd picked up when she'd bought the groceries.

One thing was for certain, she wasn't about to be caught in her tatty old sleepwear again. Wondering when Dillon was going to be home, Eleanor retired to her room, turned on her computer and took up the hunt where she'd left off.

Delilah Marie Silks. Where are you?

All week she'd searched without success. She should give up on her mother, just like Delilah had given up on her all those years ago. But Eleanor couldn't. Not anymore.

Since she'd seen the picture of Dillon and his family and the obvious love they shared, she'd developed a stubborn, burning desire to have family of her very own...to know who her mother was. Unaccountably, she wanted answers to questions that only Delilah Marie Silks could give her.

As a child, she'd stared at the name on her birth certificate, trying to imagine who Delilah was, making excuses for why her mother didn't come for her, wondering what she'd done wrong to make her mother abandon her the way she had.

Now, the more she thought about it, the more determined she was to find out about the woman who had given her life, lonely as it had been. Why had she done that? Loved someone enough to make a baby, then left that baby as soon as she was born?

It only took moments for Eleanor to lose herself in the laborious task of the Internet search. Just as quickly she lost track of time.

"Hi. You're still up."

The sound of Dillon's voice pierced Eleanor's concentration like a bullet. Instantly, she closed the screen she'd been studying so fiercely.

"Um. Yeah. I wasn't tired."

"What are you working on?"

"Just a project for work." Eleanor didn't want anyone to know she was looking for her mother, especially not the man leaning casually in her bedroom doorway as if he had nothing better to do.

His dark, wavy hair was rumpled, falling haphazardly across his forehead. His green eyes were sparkling with an emotion Eleanor wasn't sure she wanted to investigate, but responded to nonetheless. He was dressed in his usual jeans and sport coat, his tie pulled loose and hanging, as if at some time during the evening it had started to choke him. His aftershave teased Eleanor's reason and his silent regard began to make her nervous.

"Is work all you do? Don't you do anything for fun?" Annoyed, Dillon couldn't believe how many times he'd tried to talk to Eleanor during the last week and how many times she'd used the excuse of work to avoid him.

"Work is fun to me." She'd turned her back on her computer and was watching him closely, suspicion darkening her eyes.

"Do you know how to play chess?" Dillon wondered how long she was going to run from him. It was just a stupid kiss, after all. He wasn't going to say he was sorry. Not again. Besides, she couldn't be totally immune to him, if her own response was anything to go by.

"I play on the computer."

"Then you play to win. You'd beat the socks off me. Have you ever played poker?" Dillon definitely liked the confusion his question aroused. Well-shaped brows puckered thoughtfully and full lips opened slightly to play havoc with his unsatisfied desire to hold her once again and do more than kiss her.

"Poker?"

"It's a card game. Have you played it on the computer?"

"No, I've heard of it, but never played. I'm not good at cards." Eleanor's confusion disappeared, replaced by genuine interest.

"How about a game of poker, then?" There was no way Dillon was going to sleep tonight, anyway. Not with Ryan on a sleepover and the gorgeous Eleanor Rose Stone tapping on her keyboard just down the hall from him. Better to see if there was a chance he could get to know her...maybe even understand what moved the woman who'd accidentally become his wife. What better way than teaching her a simple card game?

"Sure."

For just a moment, Dillon wondered about the sudden, rare twinkle of mischief that Eleanor aimed in his direction. Instead of trying to analyze the look, he decided it would be better to ignore the way it made his body come to full attention.

"Great. I'll meet you in my office in five minutes.

By the way, I like your new flannels.'' Dillon couldn't help ribbing the woman igniting his senses—payback was good—as he slowly raked her from head to toe, unable to overlook how the soft cotton of the pj's draped suggestively over her breasts, while failing to hide the curve of her hips.

In that getup, Eleanor shouldn't have been the least bit sexy. But she was, he admitted reluctantly. Before he could do more than simply appreciate the blush that tinted her elegant cheekbones, Dillon turned to go change into more comfortable poker-playing clothes.

''Uh, Dillon?'' At the question in Eleanor's husky voice, he glanced over his shoulder. ''I should tell you. I always play to win.''

The challenge lurking in the bewitching woman's spell-binding expression made Dillon stumble. Catching himself before he could look incredibly stupid, he decided this night might just turn out to be better than he'd planned, after all.

Wearing an old pair of sweats, Dillon went to get a beer for himself and a glass of wine for his partner. Partner... Determined not to go there, he tossed away the tantalizing image the word implied. When he got to his office, Eleanor was waiting for him.

''How's your ankle?'' he asked, placing the drinks on a table between two wing chairs that reposed by the window.

''Fine. It's almost all better.'' Eleanor lounged gracefully in one chair, while Dillon went to get the deck of cards from his desk.

''No medication today?''

''None.''

''Good. Then you can have a glass of wine and

I'll explain the rules of the game." Dillon wasn't sure he'd ever seen this particular look of excitement lighting Eleanor's expression before. An internal drumroll announced he was going to enjoy this contest.

"Okay, first, poker is a betting game. We can play strip poker."

"Strip poker?"

Dillon almost laughed at Eleanor's shocked expression. Testing this woman stirred his predatory instincts. He didn't miss how it sharpened his senses, or...

"Yeah. Whoever loses a hand has to take off a piece of clothing." She would never go for it. The Eleanor he knew was way too uptight to play this game.

"Or...?"

"Or we can play for money."

Eleanor couldn't believe how tempting the man sitting across from her was. He was like a big jungle cat on the prowl. Watching. Circling. Assessing her defenses.

He challenged her more than she'd ever been in her life. She shouldn't spar with him, but he made her feel more alive, more interesting, more wanted than she'd ever felt. It was like he was trying to pull her from the darkness into the light. And she had to admit, she was interested. He teased her senses, intrigued her. He made her feel brave enough to crawl out of her cocoon and fly.

"Strip poker." Eleanor immediately wished she could bite her tongue. Crap!

Chapter Eight

Eleanor concentrated fiercely while Dillon explained the rules of the game. She didn't know how far the man was willing to go with this game, but she sure as heck wasn't planning to strip naked for him. Besides, if she was very lucky, there was a good possibility she might get to see more of her temporary husband than those sexy feet of his.

Memories of the man bested at his own game and buck-naked to boot would be good to take away with her when she had to leave. And leave she would. Eleanor stoically forced herself to remember her accidental marriage to this fascinating man couldn't last. He didn't want her. She didn't want him. Not that way.

When it came time to split, it would be much better to leave with her heart whole, not battered. In the meantime, she wouldn't mind making a few special memories.

"Are you ready? This can be a practice hand if you want."

Eleanor watched as Dillon dealt out the first hand, then picked up the cards he'd placed in front of her. An ace of hearts, two of diamonds, two of hearts, eight of spades and ten of spades.

Secretly, she glanced at the man kicking up her heartbeat, noticing that his satisfied smile had disappeared behind an indifferent mask. Only his eyebrow lifted when he looked up to find her studying him.

"How many cards do you want?"

"I'll take two," she said, discarding the eight and ten.

"I'll take one... Okay, what've you got?"

"A pair of twos." Eleanor laid her cards on the table, disappointed.

"Tough luck. I've got two pairs. Queen high. That means you get to take off an article of clothing."

Eleanor's heart squeezed at the expectant look on Dillon's face. "You said this was just a practice hand."

"Right. Okay then, your deal."

Again, Eleanor exchanged two cards. Dillon exchanged three. Again, Dillon won. Where did those three jacks come from, Eleanor wondered, frowning. Thank goodness she was wearing socks. Slowly, she pulled off the left one.

"Nice nail polish, El. My turn to deal."

Eleanor closely watched Dillon shuffle the deck and skillfully deal out five cards to each of them. He wasn't going to win, she vowed. She would never live it down if she couldn't beat this man at his own game. Already, she knew he was a better cook than she was. He was a better parent than she could ever hope to be. He was not going to be a better poker player, too.

Looking at her cards, she deliberately hid her disappointment. Nothing. Not a single pair, or run of anything. After selecting the three of clubs to keep—three was her lucky number—Eleanor ignored Dillon's Cheshire cat grin and tossed four cards on the table between them. "Give me four cards."

"I'll take two."

"I've got a pair of aces," Dillon crowed magnificently after he placed his new cards in his hand.

"That's too bad. I've got three threes." Eleanor placed the cards faceup on the table, satisfaction bubbling over her like a fountain. Delighted her lucky three had come through for her and feeling very wicked, she held out her hand and wiggled her fingers for Dillon's forfeited piece of clothing as she took a sip of her wine.

Off came a sock, a long, innocent foot, now braced on his knee, mocking her.

"Beginner's luck, El."

"Wishful thinking, Stone. My turn to deal." More challenged by this childish game than she'd ever been with all her librarian research, Eleanor hunkered down to play some serious poker.

Five hands later, Dillon was left with only his sweat bottoms and boxers, while Eleanor had only her pajama top, bra—which he occasionally got a tantalizing view of when she reached for her cards—and panties. His beer was gone and Eleanor's glass of wine was empty. He'd conceded that she could count the material thing that held her hair back as a piece of clothing, just so he could watch her hair escape its tight confines and hang around her shoulders in a long, pale curtain.

Joan had been gentle, kind and easy on the senses. The tiger that sat opposite him was competitive, aggressive and hated to lose. She sparked his own competitiveness and stirred his need to challenge her. She was deliberate and purposeful in her strategy. He wondered if she made love the same way. That thought, along with the faint scent of vanilla, captured him.

"Okay, Mrs. Stone. Let's see what you've got." *In more ways than one.*

Eyes round and startled, Eleanor laid down her cards. A straight. Two-three-four-five-six. He couldn't beat it.

Tossing his cards down, faceup, Dillon stood and slowly shimmied out of his sweatpants, aroused more by the unmistakable wonder he found lurking in Eleanor's staring regard than by the fact that he stood almost naked for the woman. Just for a second, he stood perfectly still while she checked him out from his bare chest to his...

"Plaid boxers, Mr. Stone?"

Eleanor couldn't have missed his instant reaction to her intimate perusal. A reaction Dillon wished he could have hidden when her cheeks blushed with unmistakable awareness. In that instant, he ached to have an equally clear view of her curves, instead of the pajama top hiding them.

"Your turn to deal," she said, finally taking her curious eyes off his heated body and hastily shoving her cards across the table at him.

What would she do if she won the next hand, Dillon wondered, his heartbeat still racing from the unconscious hunger she'd stroked him with. Unaccustomed wickedness stabbed at his usual honesty. He shouldn't do what he was thinking of doing. He couldn't believe he was even considering it. It had been far too long since he'd let a woman's hungry appreciation affect him so strongly. His usual good sense died a swift death.

Part of the arousing thing about Eleanor was her innocence. He didn't think she had a clue what her open regard was doing to him. Normally, her thoughts were totally hidden, but tonight, they flashed across her striking features, igniting a response he'd never in a million years believe he could have for the dedicated working-woman sitting opposite him.

He knew he should put up a better fight. But, he didn't have the strength. His lists forgotten, all Dillon could think about was seeing where all these aroused feelings were going to lead to. After all, they were two mature adults. Ryan was out of the house. And, they *were* married. That should make the natural course of their attraction okay. Right? Dillon sat back down and picked up the deck to deal the next hand.

"I'll take four cards," Eleanor said, looking disgruntled.

Dillon grinned to himself, enjoying the growing crack in his unusual wife's stoic facade. "I'll take one."

"What do you have, Stone?"

Dillon wasn't prepared for the rush of excitement that tripped him at Eleanor's attempt at nonchalant interest in his cards. She was betrayed by the nervous beating of her fingertips against the table.

"Uh...I don't have much." Dillon slowly laid

down his hand, which was nothing but an odd collection of suits and numbers.

"I have a pair of fours." Eleanor appeared to choke.

"I guess you win." Dillon had never done a provocative striptease for a woman before. Now that it was time to divest his last piece of clothing, if it wasn't for the blazing interest Eleanor was trying so desperately to hide, he was pretty sure there was no way in the world he could have pulled off the stunt he was planning.

"Okay. Wait." Eleanor jumped up while he was still trying to figure out how to perform the striptease, his thumbs stuck in the band of his boxers. "You don't have to do that. Let's just agree I won. I'll take my things and go up to my room. No problem. It was a great game. Maybe we can do it again sometime."

Watching Eleanor straighten her glasses, Dillon choked back a surprised chuckle as she pulled her hair severely back into its ponytail, then jerked her pajama top down when she suddenly realized the short garment had slipped up, giving him a bird's-eye view of soft blue, silky underwear. Blushing an intriguing shade of pink, she grabbed her clothes from the floor and pulled on one sock, while hopping around the coffee table.

"Um…are you sure? A bet is a bet, you know." Dillon didn't bother to resist the overwhelming inclination he had to tease the funny woman who frantically tried to escape the room. The last thing he saw of Eleanor Rose Stone was long, lithe legs—one droopy sock on, the other lost on the carpet at his feet—dashing up the stairs as if all the Baskerville's hounds were after her.

Picking up the discarded sock, Dillon watched her disappear, the irony of the whole situation hitting him broadside. First, he'd set out to find a mother for Ryan and a comfortable wife for himself. He'd gotten Eleanor Rose, instead. Now he found himself totally, impossibly attracted to the wife he didn't want, and he couldn't keep her in the same room with him for more than a moment of not-so-frivolous flirtation. Wife? Why in the world had he acknowledged that fact by calling her Mrs. Stone?

Maybe he should just admit himself to the Bellevue Mental Hospital. That would be a whole lot easier than coming up with reasons not to explore their mutual attraction to its natural conclusion.

Oh, hell. If they had sex just once, it wouldn't mean anything, would it?

It would mean Eleanor wouldn't get her annulment, a little voice reminded him, nastily.

Well, maybe he didn't want to give her that annulment. Dillon shook his head. What was he thinking? Of course he wanted to give her the annulment. Didn't he?

Dillon closed his eyes in frustration. The only sure thing in his life right now was that he needed another cold shower. It would only be the sixth one he'd taken that week.

He'd called her Mrs. Stone. Eleanor leaned weakly against the bedroom door, reliving again the hungry look in Dillon's eyes as he started to drop his drawers. She'd been so distracted by the sight of dark, curling hair on his chest, she'd almost missed that last hand, and the fact that she'd won the game, and that Dillon had been very prepared to pay up his debt.

How could he do that to her? Did he *want* to strip naked for her? Eleanor's heart pounded in her chest and she suddenly couldn't breathe.

Get a grip, girl. Just because the man kissed you, doesn't mean he wants to strip naked for you. He's just being...

Eleanor didn't know what he was being, but *nice* wasn't a word she would use to describe Dillon Stone at this moment. Responsible, yes. Sexy as sin, yes. Nice, no.

Pushing away from the door, Eleanor flopped on the bed, staring at the ceiling. It was pure blind luck winning that last hand. Poker was more a game of chance than she'd first realized. Never in her wildest dreams had she imagined that Dillon Stone's body would be so...so...*male*. This intense attraction she had for him had to stop. She would never make it out of this house in one piece if she didn't stop allowing the irresistible man inroads into her heart.

Dillon Stone did not love her. He still loved Joan. She had to remember that. He didn't want a working, corporate, doesn't-know-how-to-cook woman like her. He wanted a domestic, homemaker-type, like Joan. The type of woman Eleanor had actually taken a lot of pains to avoid becoming.

That depressing thought was making it impossible to sleep. She may as well get back to her "Delilah search," as she'd come to think of her sudden, confusing need to find her mother.

The next morning, after very little sleep, Eleanor crept down the stairs. With Ryan gone, the house was too quiet. It seemed an impossible feat, but the little boy had wormed his way into her heart and was standing right next to his father in a secret place she had never allowed anyone to enter.

Stick to the plan, no matter what!

Sometime in the early hours, when she wasn't sleeping but only seeing images of laughing eyes, a strong, bare, masculine chest, and imagining quite successfully what was hiding under those crazy plaid boxers, Eleanor had decided she was going to move out. She couldn't risk her heart any further by staying in Dillon's house.

Hopefully it wasn't too late. She had too much to lose. She wasn't sure why she'd let Dillon talk her into moving in with him in the first place. An insane impulse. A momentary surrender to an impossible adolescent crush she thought long ago resolved. But now, being in such close proximity with the man only resurrected those feelings and burned them hotter.

A soft sound stopped Eleanor as she reached the bottom of the stairs. Rubbing her palms nervously against her pant legs, she glanced into the living room, finding the man occupying her thoughts to the exclusion of all else, stretched out on the couch. One arm draped across his bare chest, the other dangled, his fingertips resting on an old, leather-bound book lying on the floor.

At the sight of him peacefully sleeping, Eleanor's heart turned over. How was she going to make herself live without the dratted man? His thick, wavy hair stuck out in wild disarray, as if he'd been pushing his fingers repeatedly through the heavy strands.

His usually rugged features were softened in sleep, giving him the slightly boyish look Eleanor remembered. He slept with his mouth slightly open... inviting.

A soft snore escaped, capturing Eleanor's dancing senses. How could a snore be seductive?

Eleanor bent to pick up the book, trying to ignore the hair sprinkling Dillon's chest and the way it led her appreciative eye to the waistband of his jeans. The top button was open, revealing dark blue...more boxers?

Careful not to disturb him, Eleanor slid the book away and picked it up, curious what kind of reading material kept the man so engaged, he'd fallen asleep on the couch.

The smell of soap mixed with man fragrance reminded Eleanor she'd heard the shower after she'd rushed up to her room last night. Vaguely, she remembered reading once that women chose their mates by smell and had to remind herself she wasn't one of them.

Absently opening the book, Eleanor plunked down into the overstuffed chair she'd backed into and read the opening lines of what appeared to be a diary. The page was faded, but she could easily make out the dainty writing.

This is the diary of Savannah Marie Silks, started on this day, September 10, 1896....

"Oh, my God. I don't believe it," Eleanor croaked, grabbing up the suddenly ringing phone on the coffee table. Her glance darted between the diary lying where she'd dropped it in her lap and the man beginning to stir on the couch opposite her.

"Stone residence," she snapped. What was going on here?

"El? Is that you?" Jake's familiar voice came faintly over the line.

"Jake? I can't hear you very well. Where are you?" It was the first time he'd been in touch since her so-called wedding. Knowing that he never contacted her while he was away on assignment made her suddenly anxious. "Are you okay? You're not hurt, are you?"

"Hang on a minute. I'm on a da...ce...one. Is that better?" Jake finally asked, his voice abruptly crystal clear, as if he were phoning from the next room.

"Better."

"Listen, El. I don't have much time. I'm not hurt. I just wanted to check to see how you and Dillon are getting along...."

At the mention of his name, Eleanor looked up to find Dillon watching her, his earlier sleepy gaze disturbingly wide-awake.

"Your phone was disconnected and I got worried. I decided to try Dillon's on the off-chance you'd be there. Does this mean you're still married?" Jake's amused curiosity irritated Eleanor, since from where she stood, her current predicament was partly his fault.

Hunching her shoulder and lowering her voice in a doomed attempt for some privacy, Eleanor turned away from Dillon's steady curiosity. "Not exactly."

Strong fingers squeezing her knee grabbed her attention immediately. Eleanor looked up to see Dillon studying her intently, his distracting mouth moving in a brief whisper, causing more than just waves of sound to reach her ears.

"I'll go make us breakfast."

Eleanor nodded, struck again by the sight of his strong, bare chest, and when he turned to leave the room, the way his back molded perfectly to his hips and...

"El, are you there?"

"Sure."

"So, give me the scoop," Jake demanded teasingly.

Eleanor forced herself to concentrate on her foster brother, reluctantly explaining the circumstances that had brought her to Dillon's home. She told him about the zoo accident. Her cheeks burning, she didn't tell him about the strip poker.

When she'd finished, for a moment Jake was too quiet on the other end of the line.

"It sounds like you like him, El."

"Of course I like him. What's not to like? He's a good parent."

"It's more than like, El. Something's going on. Sounds like you might lo—"

"Jake. You and I both know that sappy kind of ever-after love does not exist in this world. And, whatever's left doesn't make people stick around when you need them the most."

"I love you, El." Jake's voice was soft, sincere.

"I love you, too, brat, but that has nothing to do with Dillon Stone and you know it."

"El. I didn't mean to get you married to Dillon. But now that you are, it's an opportunity to walk away from your past. Don't let it scare you. It's time to start over, make a new life and let lasting love be a part of it."

"What do you know about starting over?"

Eleanor asked warily, not believing for a minute anything Jake Solomon was saying. Her foster brother had never stayed with a woman more than a month, himself. How could he know what he was talking about?

"I loved a girl once, El. But I made a mistake and let her get away. I regret that. Next time I won't be so stupid. Don't be afraid. You have to love to be loved."

"You're full of the wrong advice today, Jake. Dillon and I are getting an annulment. There's not a chance in...well, he doesn't love me and I don't love him. Besides, he still loves Joan," Eleanor said frankly, trying hard to accept the truth of it.

"I've got to go. I won't be able to call again, but promise me you won't give Dillon up without a fight. Promise me you'll give whatever's between you a fighting chance."

"There is nothing between us and I'm not making you any promises I can't keep. You're asking me to believe in the impossible." Eleanor wasn't going to allow Jake to push her into anything. She was used to him trying to run her life, but this was one time it couldn't be allowed.

"I'm not asking for you to believe in the impossible. I'm just asking you to believe in you. Promise, El. You owe me."

"So, I *owe* you?" She would not promise Jake anything. She recognized his sigh of resignation.

"Love you, sis. At least take care of yourself while I'm gone." Jake's soft emotion was replaced by the disconnect buzz as Dillon appeared in the doorway.

"Breakfast is ready."

                          *   *   *

He shouldn't have eavesdropped on Eleanor's conversation with Jake.

Dillon and I are getting an annulment, she'd told her brother. Wasn't that what he wanted, too? Dillon placed two plates of omelets on the table next to the glasses of orange juice he'd poured earlier.

After last night, he wasn't sure what he wanted.

He doesn't love me and I don't love him. She'd sure gotten that right. But that last part... Eleanor thought he still loved Joan. Of course he did. He would always have special feelings for his college sweetheart and the mother of his son. That didn't mean he couldn't find companionship with another woman, did it? His heart didn't have to be involved. He just needed to find someone he could live comfortably with and who would be a good mother to Ryan. Taking a chance on falling in love again had never been in his plan at all.

"That was Jake."

As she sat at the table, Dillon wasn't surprised by the wary look on Eleanor's face. He wondered if it had anything to do with Jake's call or was just a leftover from their game of strip poker. Dillon pushed away the memory of pale blue panties and long, long legs.

"How's Jake doing?"

"He's okay."

"What did he want?" Dillon persisted, curious at Eleanor's silence. Not that she was big on conversation, anyway.

"He wanted to know how we were getting along."

"Did you tell him we're getting along fine?" Dillon sat down at the table opposite Eleanor and

watched with interest as she stabbed at the omelet
he'd placed in front of her.

"El?"

"I told him we're working on an annulment."

Not knowing what to make of the brief look of
dejection that was instantly replaced by studied indifference, Dillon sat back, his appetite suddenly
gone.

"Is that what you want?" he asked harshly of the
woman avoiding his direct gaze.

"Yes. Of course it is." Finally, lifting her chin in
that defiant little gesture of hers, Eleanor matched
him glare for glare.

How could he be so attracted to the woman and
at the same time be so damn mad at her? Dillon
pushed his plate of untouched food away as a shrill
brrring suddenly interrupted the drop-dead silence
between them. On the third persistent ring, he
grabbed the phone off the wall. "Hello?" he barked.

"Hey, son."

"Pop." Dillon took a deep breath, trying to sep-
arate himself from his unreasonable emotions. It was
dangerous to his peace of mind to let himself get so
involved with Eleanor.

"I'm thinking about flying out for a visit next
week," his dad said gruffly, his voice effectively distracting him from the infuriating woman opposite
him. Long eyelashes hid those blazing eyes as she
studied the food she was pushing restlessly around
her plate.

"Next week might not be such good timing, Pop."

"Why, is something wrong? Is Ryan okay?"

Dillon had long ago given up trying to keep secrets
from his dad. The old man's ability to figure out

when his son or grandson was in trouble was uncanny. "No, we're both fine. But Ryan is in a new school and I have to prepare for my classes."

"I still don't understand why you had to give up being a criminal lawyer," his father grumbled.

"I told you, Pop, working in the courtroom kept me away from Ryan. This way, I will basically be on the same schedule he is. It's bad enough he doesn't have his mother anymore. The least I can do is make sure his dad is around."

After a short silence, his dad gave a tired sigh. "You're right, of course, son. I just miss you guys. I think I'll come out, anyway. I won't get in your way. I just want to see for myself that my grandson is settling into his new home okay. I'll try to let you know before I come." And before Dillon could stop him, his dad had hung up.

Hanging up the phone, Dillon realized Eleanor had slipped out unnoticed during his conversation with his father. The last thing he wanted was for his sentimental old man to get a load of Eleanor...and the fact that she was his wife, even if it was only temporary. He remembered what his dad had told him as a teenager, shortly after his own mother had died.

Love and the perfect partner are hard commodities to come by.

"Where did you find this book?" The woman stomping like a bull through his thoughts suddenly reappeared holding up the old diary he'd found at the university library.

In her hands, Eleanor held her first clue to finding Delilah Marie Silks. A fragile hope buffeted her almost as much as Jake's impossible fairy tale of love. Following clues until she found what she was looking for was what she did best. She couldn't believe she'd run across the odd reference to her family name just when she so desperately needed to leave.

When Dillon looked at her blankly, Eleanor explained, "This diary." Carefully, she held up the fragile book so Dillon could see what she was talking about. "Where did you get it?"

"Silks is an unusual name. I stopped by the campus library yesterday after the faculty meeting to see what I could find. The head librarian there collects historical biographies."

Ignoring the thoughtful frown pulling Dillon's brows together, Eleanor reluctantly placed the rare book in his outstretched hand. How could she leave just now? When she'd found a reference—even though it was a remote possibility—that could lead to her mother.

Swallowing the emotional lump sticking in her throat, Eleanor pushed her glasses farther up her nose and moved to look over Dillon's elbow as he carefully opened the book.

This is the diary of Savannah Marie Silks....

Dillon's gentle touch on the yellowed page stabbed Eleanor with a lightening strike, suddenly reminding her just how much she liked it when he touched her in the same thoughtful, protective way.

Ruthlessly, she closed her heart to the longing that ran like a stampeding herd over her. She was a logical, realistic and responsible person. It was time to stop being so emotional.

"My full name is Eleanor...Silks...Rose."

"I know."

Chapter Nine

"My mother's name is Delilah Marie Silks."

"When I ran across this, I wondered if there could be a connection." Leverage. It was just what Dillon needed. Now that he had it, what was he going to do with it?

"Why do you care?"

Dillon understood what was going through Eleanor's mind. He'd been a teenager when his mother died, and he'd been blindly angry at what he'd considered her desertion. How often had he wondered what he'd done that was so wrong that God had decided to take her away from him?

"Is this the first time you've tried to find your mom? It isn't your fault she left you in the hospital." He wasn't sure himself why he cared, but suddenly he did. A great deal.

Dillon tried not to think about the way Eleanor stood so straight and still, staring at the diary as if it held the greatest secret in the world. She'd notched her chin up as if by doing so he wouldn't see how much she was affected by his discovery.

Whatever it was, it didn't surprise him when Eleanor took a step back, separating herself from the emotions that flared briefly in eyes that glared, daring him to cross the invisible line she was drawing in the sand between them.

He'd come to expect the protective walls she persistently erected around herself. What he hadn't expected was his need to chip away at them until they came tumbling down. Had this beautiful woman always been so alone? Dillon wondered, his protective instincts leaping to full attention.

"I haven't tried until...recently." Clearly she didn't want to discuss her mother.

Catching the faint scent of vanilla that was specifically Eleanor's, Dillon found himself unable to take his eyes off her. Lost in unsteady emotions, he maneuvered one step closer, not wanting the clever woman to find the hiding place she was frantically searching for.

"Is that why you're at your keyboard until the early hours of the morning? It isn't work at all, is it? It's this search for your mom." Dillon treasured the memories he had of his mother. Was it possible he could help the woman stopping his advance with both hands pushing against his chest?

"El..." Dillon reached for Eleanor's face and found himself touching only air.

Eleanor was backing down the hall, her hand raised to ward him off. He watched those whiskey eyes close and her expression become bleak, and his heart sank at her withdrawal.

"I don't need or want your pity, Dillon Stone,"

she spat at him like a cornered, frightened kitten. Then she turned on her heel and started for the stairs.

Unfortunately, pity had nothing to do with the aroused feelings the sight of his dating-game wife conjured up. He wished pity was all he had to deal with. This time, for her own good, he wasn't going to let her get away with her usual habit of running away from him.

Swallowing his frustration, Dillon followed Eleanor up the stairs, barely able to keep up with her.

"El, I can help." He had to practically shout to get the fleeing woman to stop her headlong flight and listen to him.

"I don't want your help," she said, not turning to face him.

Dillon admired the little spitfire's damned independent nature, but a person could take self-reliance a bit too far. "There might be something in the diary that can help you find your mother."

He held his breath as Eleanor reached the landing and slowly turned to stare at the book he was dangling in front of her cute nose, hoping to get her attention. He did.

And it was worth it when stubborn defiance changed to wary interest. Why did he care that the woman hesitantly moving toward him and the book he held out like a carrot was so alone in the world? She didn't want his help. She didn't want to be married to him. Did he or did he not want to be married to her?

The solution was simple. Give her the annulment she wanted so badly and be done with her. Dillon grimaced as if he'd heard fingernails being scratched down a chalkboard.

"This diary might give you a place to start." He tempted the wary woman again and got the results he wanted when she moved close enough to reach out and take the lifeline he was offering.

Eleanor wondered why she was doing this to herself. She should be packing her bags and leaving.

"Savannah could be your long-lost ancestor." Dillon's deep, seductive voice wrapped around her, tempting Eleanor to forget for a moment that all she wanted was to leave this place, leave behind this man who stood, hands on hips in the small hallway, challenging her to accept what he had to offer—his son, a home with them and the scary feeling of not wanting to be alone anymore.

"I don't know why I started looking for her. It's not like she's ever cared about what happened to me." Whispering her secret belief, Eleanor didn't notice that Dillon had closed the gap between them until his arm draped gently around her shoulders.

"I think it's natural to want to know our parents, no matter who they are or what they've done. Maybe there was a valid reason for your mother leaving you at the hospital." Dillon's touch made her shiver with something that had absolutely nothing to do with their current conversation.

"Maybe, but what kind of mother would abandon her child for any reason?" Eleanor choked back the bitterness that threatened her.

When Dillon shook her slightly, sympathy etching the rugged planes of his face, shivers scratched down Eleanor's back as his voice spoke gruffly near her ear. "It could have been as simple as not being able to take care of you."

Arrested, Eleanor leaned back, wishing desperately she could believe Dillon. "It's more likely she didn't want a baby in the first place and didn't know what to do with one once she got me."

"You can't know that." The look of devastating isolation on Eleanor's face was more than Dillon could stand.

"No circumstance in the world, no matter how bleak, would induce me to leave my child to be raised by strangers." Eleanor spoke fiercely.

Moved beyond expression, he wiped away the lone tear that slid down her pale cheek with his thumb. He was stunned by the glimpse of the circumstances that had made Eleanor into such a formidable woman.

Careful, so he wouldn't give her reason to bolt, Dillon turned her toward him, cupping each side of her face, his thumbs settling over her cheekbones. Pulling her close, he dived recklessly into drowning whiskey eyes and thought…what…? That he could offer something she'd never had?

"I know you would never abandon your baby." Dillon's throat clutched at the image of Eleanor's belly swollen…with his child. "Let me help you find your mother. Between the two of us, we can do it," he whispered, unable to resist the image of the two of them working together…spending intimate time together.

Moving his hands to her shoulder, Dillon tugged Eleanor close to his heart and went for what he wanted. One illicit, thought-blocking kiss.

Of course, that was all he wanted, he reassured

himself as a persistent voice shouted in his mind. If you keep Eleanor busy searching for her mother, maybe she'll forget that blasted annulment.

Gently, he brushed his lips across hers until they softened and opened with welcome. When her hands grabbed the bare skin at his waist, Dillon realized he was standing on an emotional cliff and a jump off the edge could be very dangerous.

Taking a deep breath to calm his racing heart, he broke lip-contact before his flaming senses overrode his good intentions. Dillon dropped his forehead against Eleanor's, unreasonably savoring the look of dreamy distraction flickering across her delicate features.

"Bring the diary and come back to the kitchen. Read to me, while I clean up the breakfast dishes," he demanded softly. If he was doing something as mundane as washing dishes, he might have a good chance of saving himself and stepping away from the cliff's edge.

"Ryan wants you to tuck him into bed." Dillon leaned in Eleanor's bedroom doorway, interrupting her study of Savannah's diary.

He hadn't seen her since he'd left earlier in the day to pick up his son. She'd been so buried in the diary, he was sure she hadn't even noticed he'd left. That her lack of attention irritated the heck out of him was too comical.

Even now she had a faraway look in her eyes, as if she was still lost in Savannah's story and having trouble understanding what he'd said to her.

"El…"

"Okay, I'm coming." She quickly slipped the

book under her pillow, surprising Dillon with a flush that warmed her skin to a pretty rose color.

She didn't look at him when she slipped by and disappeared into Ryan's room. The warm cadence of her voice soothed his ragged nerves just as he was sure it was soothing his son.

Ryan loved Eleanor. It was plain to see how the little guy felt. What was he going to tell his son when the woman he wanted to be his new mom finally figured out her accidental husband hadn't filed the annulment papers, like she'd told him to? She would leave them.

The sharp pain that stabbed him in the region of his heart shocked Dillon. How could he possibly let this confounding, contradicting, irritating woman go? And when he did, how was he going to stop the hurt that was inevitable for Ryan?

Dillon stuffed his hands in his back pockets and leaned against the wall outside his son's door. He really didn't know what to do about their unusual situation. He should just file like Eleanor wanted. Why hadn't he taken care of it already?

Exasperated, he started a new list in his mind.

Eleanor was stubborn. She didn't like to cook. She was messy and didn't clean up after herself. She continually left her coat lying on the couch and never took her clean clothes out of the dryer.

She definitely wasn't a Suzie Homemaker. She hid from the world behind glasses, he noted, remembering her habit of pushing the wire rims up her nose when her emotions were high. She wanted an annulment. But she clearly cared for his son.

"Good night, Ryan."

Dillon was surprised by the tears that sparkled in

Eleanor's eyes when she came out of Ryan's room. She pushed on the bridge of the glasses in a purely defensive gesture, attempting again to hide her emotions from him. And before he could stop himself, he plucked the lenses from her face, earning a shocked gasp for his efforts.

"You hide behind these things. Why?" Dillon held them up to the light considering the minuscule change in the lenses.

"I don't hide behind anything. I need them to read. Give those back to me." Making a frustrated sound, Eleanor tried to snatch her glasses back, but Dillon prudently held them out of reach as he raised a cocky eyebrow at her.

She realized too soon that attempting to grab her glasses meant plastering her body against his, smashing tantalizing breasts to his chest. Stepping back, she held out her hand.

"This is silly. Give them to me."

"Silly?" Dillon frowned. Yeah. He guessed it was pretty juvenile.

"I'll give them back if you'll come have popcorn with me." Dillon felt like a playground bully, but for reasons he didn't dare explore, he wasn't willing to let Eleanor slip away to a place where he was not welcome.

"Blackmail is against the law, Dillon Stone."

"Yeah. I guess it is. Meet me in the living room and bring Savannah's diary with you." With those commands, the man spun on his bare feet, taking Eleanor's glasses with him, and left her standing, gawking after him like a lovesick teenager.

Released from Dillon's powerful magnetism, Eleanor tried to figure out what had just happened.

Dillon Stone had stolen her glasses. Stolen them! Of course she didn't hide behind them. That was a stupid accusation. She only needed them to read. Suddenly, Eleanor wished for the days when her life wasn't so complicated and her emotions weren't so stirred up by one irritating, insolent law professor.

She wasn't going to let him get away with this. So far, Savannah's diary hadn't really told her much. She should probably just give it back to him but she wasn't ready to. Mr. Stone was not going to be allowed to get away with bullying and commanding her into doing what he wanted.

From what little she'd read, Eleanor found she admired Savannah Silks, ancestor or not. She was a woman who'd built a place for herself in the new western frontier, where life was tough. She had a strength and fortitude that Eleanor could only envy, because she wasn't that way herself.

Squaring her shoulders, Eleanor buried the surviving picture of her traitorous body pressed so close to Dillon's. She didn't think even a thin piece of paper could have been slipped between them. The memory of that kiss in her bedroom was still hot enough to singe the ends of her hair.

What would Savannah do? She would take control of the situation, that's what she'd do. Taking the diary with her, Eleanor started down the stairs to give Dillon what-for in pure Silks style. Then she would pack her bags and leave.

Dillon popped the pouch of popcorn in the microwave, wondering why he was doing this. Had he lost his mind? Eleanor obviously didn't want his interference. But, when she purposely closed herself off to him...she became an irresistible contradiction and made him forget he was a reasonable and sensible guy.

His growing need to be near her, to touch her, to claim her as his own, greatly troubled Dillon. He was not some barbarian who didn't know how to behave around a lady. But there were times when Eleanor made him feel barbaric, wanting only to scoop her up, throw her over his shoulder and take her to his lair. It didn't make any sense. He was a lawyer, for God's sake, moved only by facts and logic.

Dillon pulled the popcorn out of the microwave as the timer went off. His thoughts locked on the problem that was Eleanor Silks Rose Stone, he shook the bag so the kernels wouldn't burn.

Was he admitting he was over-the-moon attracted to Eleanor—who also, very conveniently, happened to be his wife? Was he saying that, despite all their differences and how totally opposite from the women on his lists she was, he—for some unexplained reason—wanted to keep Eleanor? As his wife? This wasn't high school and Eleanor wasn't a new truck he could keep just because he'd suddenly decided he wanted to.

Dillon couldn't forget how his body hardened when he molded her softness against him and how she responded to his kisses when she forgot who she was fighting. He almost chuckled out loud at the memory of her embarrassment when he'd tried to strip to his next-to-nothings after their infamous poker game, and her subsequent faster-than-a-bullet exit to avoid seeing his most manly possession.

Always making his life decisions based on sound reasoning, even when he'd married Joan, Dillon didn't like the confusing feelings pushing him. Marrying Joan had been as natural as taking his next breath. Marrying Eleanor had been a regretfully unanticipated mistake.

But she fascinated him. What he felt for his dating-game bride was primitive. Volcanic. Definitely possessive. Maybe, even…obsessive. Never in a thousand years would he have guessed he'd want to play Prince Charming to Eleanor's Sleeping Beauty. His whole existence was being reduced to a badly written fairy tale.

Dillon frowned. He was a rational man. He solved his problems by thinking them through, starting at the beginning and brainstorming until he found a solution. Patting the pocket where he'd carefully put her glasses, Dillon carried the snack-loaded tray into the living room, actually surprised to find Eleanor waiting.

On second glance, it didn't look as if she planned to make his evening very easy. Her expression begged for retribution as her dessert of choice. Dillon wasn't prepared for the explosive heat that nearly tripped him. Never taking his eyes off the smoldering woman, he placed the tray on the coffee table, then sat as far to the other end of the couch as he could get.

Okay. The battle lines were drawn, Dillon acknowledged, suddenly anticipating the wrestle for power that was about to take place.

"Did you find anything useful in the diary?" Dillon asked cheerfully, a long drink of beer helping to quench one thirst.

"My glasses…"

Dillon filled a paper cup with popcorn, contrariness making him brush Eleanor's fingers when he passed the popped kernels, along with her glasses into her waiting hand. Maybe he should rethink his position on their marriage, Dillon decided as he silently watched a flush of victory climb to eyes that locked in serious challenge with his.

"I haven't found anything, but the diary is giving me an idea or two." Eleanor took a deep breath, silently cursing the butterflies trying to escape her stomach by way of her constricted throat.

She was in control of this situation, not these riotous emotions that became more chaotic every time she spent more than two seconds with the man looking at her, as if he was about to divine her deepest, darkest secret.

Eleanor reported in her best corporate voice to the man watching her. "At the time that Savannah wrote the diary, she owned and operated Savannah Silks Boarding House in Shaniko, Oregon. She didn't have any children. She had a brother named Beauregard William Silks, who had a son, William Richard, born in 1910. There's nothing after that."

Dillon's gaze was intense and uninformative. A friction of familiar awareness scurried out of control, grabbing her undivided attention.

"That's at least a beginning. Maybe you can find your mother by tracing William's descendants," he suggested, dropping his gaze to stare at the piece of popcorn he was holding as if undecided what he was going to do with it.

Eleanor didn't have a good feeling about the look that darkened his incredible eyes or the suggestive glance he gave her lips. Lips that were beginning to go dry in reckless anticipation.

When the popcorn started moving toward her, Eleanor panicked. "Dillon Stone, don't you dare feed me that."

Heavy, dark brows raised in mock innocence.

"Why?"

Was the man crazy?

"Because I don't need you to feed me. If I want to eat some popcorn, I'll help myself," Eleanor informed him firmly, only to be poleaxed by the soft inquiry in his baritone voice that attempted to rub her senses into submission.

"Are you sure?"

"Of course I'm sure. I'm not a child." Despite her denial, shivers of agitated anticipation prowled through Eleanor's body.

"That's too bad. You're missing out on one of the best things in life."

Mesmerized by the hidden promise in Dillon's soft words, Eleanor lost track of the popcorn and her refusal to be fed until Dillon knocked gently on her lips with the offensive treat. By then, it was too late to refuse. Like a baby bird getting nourishment from its parent, her lips opened and the morsel was popped inside.

All that was left to do was chew and savor the treat that had been touched by the reckless man's fingers. Catching the brimming amusement in Dillon's expression, Eleanor realized she had to get out of there. Fast. Before she lost any defenses she might have left. Already, she was starting to forget why she had to pack her things and leave.

But, again, she was too late. Somehow, anticipating her decision to escape, Dillon closed the distance between them, grabbed her wrist and gently held her next to him as if he could chain her there by the strongest iron. He could.

"What's the matter? Are you scared?"

"I'm not scared of anything, Dillon Stone."

"Then prove it, Eleanor Rose Stone." Dillon tossed the challenge as he kept Eleanor close to him, liking the way her chin picked it up and tossed it back at him. "Sit here with me and share my popcorn. Tell me about your mother. Let me help you find her."

Would she let him into her life? Dillon watched her close her brilliant eyes, wary pain etching her features just for a moment. Gently, he rubbed the pounding pulse in her wrist to let her know he was there for her.

He wanted Eleanor to let him help her. And, God help him, for reasons he couldn't explain, he desperately needed to.

Feeling her tension release like an uncoiling spring, his own uncertainty left him and he moved with Eleanor as she leaned back into the couch, opening her eyes to study him coolly, her mask of control firmly back in place.

"There's nothing to say about my mother you don't already know. She deserted me at the hospital just after I was born. I only know her name. And, for some godforsaken reason, I've taken it into my head to find her. So far, no luck. It's not an unusual story and not that earth-shattering. If I can't find her, I won't die. I've lived my whole life so far without her."

Dillon stared at Eleanor, stunned. At that moment, he wondered if he could have a real marriage with this very vulnerable woman. For the first time since he'd found himself erroneously married to her, she'd honestly shared an intimate piece of herself. It was the longest personal insight he'd ever heard her utter. She knocked his socks off. She needed someone to care for her. And for the briefest moment, he wondered if it was going to be him.

Love? The emotions churning in his chest baffled him. He'd never planned to find love again. And he certainly wasn't expecting to find it with the woman whose pulse was pounding beneath his thumb. The emotions he felt for Eleanor were rocky and unbelievably gripping. But they couldn't be love.

"I want to help," he repeated. "With two of us working on it, we're bound to come up with something."

"I don't need help, Dillon."

"Yes, you do." Dillon was determined not to be shaken off so easily.

"I don't."

"You sound like a stubborn little girl."

"I'm not stubborn, and I'm not a little girl."

"You've got that right. You're not a little girl." Dillon laughed at Eleanor's surprised look and popped another popcorn in her open mouth. Emphasizing his point, he leaned close and brushed a soft, lingering kiss across her throat, fighting his desire to stay and taste deeper.

"But I'm not stubborn," the minx continued to argue.

"No?"

"No."

"Then let me be your research assistant." Dillon placed the challenge before her. Would she accept it, or toss his offer aside?

"You're pushing," Eleanor mumbled, faint pink warming her cheeks.

"Uh-huh." All he could think of was kissing Eleanor until her toes curled, but instead he planted a chaste kiss on her forehead to seal their deal. Dillon shifted, placing his lips at the corner of her eye, on the pulse that ran beneath her temple. Excitement blasted him at the tremble he felt briefly beneath his lips.

"Everyone needs someone, sometime." Tugging aside her silky hair, Dillon pressed a kiss to her enticing ear, overwhelmed by the surge of pounding desire that pulsed through him when she hesitantly tilted her head, giving him more room to explore the delicate, shell-like feature that momentarily held his attention.

"You don't need…" Her voice was deep…distracted.

That's right. He didn't need…

Shocked by his conflicting emotions, Dillon hastily stood, releasing Eleanor as if she were a wounded lioness out to claw him to protect her open wounds. He had to stop and think. Figure out a new game plan. Fast. Before he lost all logical reason. He had to stick to the plan of finding a good mother for Ryan and a comfortable companion for himself.

Eleanor? Comfortable? Not even likely.

"I've got some paperwork to do. Thanks for sharing popcorn with me," Dillon blurted hastily, knowing he sounded like a moron but unable to help it. This whole thing with Eleanor was way out of control. How could he possibly be thinking about keeping her for his wife?

"What about the diary?" Startled disbelief and confusion colored Eleanor's expression.

"We'll get together on that tomorrow." Dillon was beginning to have sympathy for Eleanor. She probably thought his actions bordered on insanity, one minute kissing her, insisting she should let him help her. The next, running as fast as he could, deserting her. He was no better than... It was insanity, that's what it was.

He had to make sense out of his escalating emotions, and he apparently wasn't going to do that while he had his arms wrapped tightly around the irresistible woman. When he was with her, all he wanted was to touch her...explore her secret places. One taste of her and he was lost. Turning on his heel, Dillon made a beeline for his office, closing the door firmly behind him, so the beautiful, whiskey-eyed blonde could not disturb him.

Chapter Ten

Hours later, Dillon still sat brooding at his desk. Slowly, he reread the list he'd meticulously assembled.

Successful businesswoman.
A workaholic.
Not domestic.
Doesn't cook real meals.
Has strong defenses—doesn't want anyone to get close.
Loves Ryan.
Loves the zoo.
Makes great-tasting chocolate-chip cookies.
Has long, silky hair.
When moved to passion, eyes turn the color of well-aged whiskey.
Has strong feelings about family.
Would make a great mother.
Makes me want to reconsider my bachelor status.
Wants marriage annulled.

Dillon knew better than to romanticize their situation. In many respects, Eleanor was right. He hadn't wanted to marry her because he loved her, nor had she wanted to marry him. The whole thing had been a mistake, the result of cosmic misadventure.

Why was he thinking about changing the playing field now? Why was he thinking about something in the category of ''forever'' with the impossible woman?

Dillon was hesitant to explore the new feelings taking over his heart every time he was near Eleanor. The more he thought about it, the more he was certain those feelings had nothing to do with love. Relief tumbled through his mind. Obviously, there was a huge difference between feelings of attraction and the feelings of love that bound a man body and soul to a certain woman.

Drawing interlocking geometric shapes on his paper, Dillon almost missed the knock at his front door. Glancing at the clock on his desk, he pocketed his new list before going to see who could be knocking at eleven o'clock at night.

On the third whack, Dillon jerked open his front door. ''Pop, what are you doing here?''

''I'm glad to see you, too, son. Let an old man in and I'll tell you all about it.''

Dillon's last thought was to wonder if his life could get any more complicated. He hadn't told his dad about Eleanor, and for good reason. He wasn't exactly embarrassed, but who would believe a tale of an accidental marriage? He guessed now, the cat would definitely get out of the bag. His dad would laugh until his sides ached.

* * *

The next morning, Eleanor woke to muffled laughter. She felt washed-out and as if she'd slept on a pea all night long.

The snap of Dillon's office door the night before had finally released her from the stunned surprise that had tied her to her seat when the infuriating man abandoned her to riotous arousal. She'd been so busy running from Dillon, she'd never given any consideration to what he might want until she'd seen his back disappearing down the hall.

Not wanting to face him, Eleanor slowly showered and dressed in a bright yellow T-shirt and blue jeans. She even decided to change the color of her nail polish from pale pink to hot power-red before she realized what a coward she was being.

She wasn't afraid of one tall, good-looking law professor, was she? Of course she wasn't. She'd never let cowardice rule her decisions before now. And, she wasn't about to start.

The sound of Dillon's laughter mocked her. There was no reason why she should be hiding in her room. Besides, she was hungry, and if she was really nice to the man, she could probably talk him into making her one of his amazing omelets.

Straightening to her tallest height, Eleanor marched herself down the stairs and straight into the kitchen, not stopping until she ran into the astonishing sight and sound of a stranger sitting at the table with Ryan.

"There's my new mom, Grandpa." Ryan squirmed out of his grandfather's arms to throw his little body snugly against hers, wrapping his sturdy arms around her waist.

Eleanor hugged the child close, not accustomed to the feelings of maternal possession that stormed over her. She glanced at the elderly man Ryan had called "Grandpa," and saw that Dillon stood behind him poised over the stove, his eyebrows raised as he watched her.

"Your new mama?" Grandpa was a rugged-looking elderly gentleman, with thick graying hair, bushy gray eyebrows and the most perfectly trimmed salt-and-pepper mustache she'd ever seen. Somewhere in his late sixties, Ryan's grandfather could still turn the ladies' heads. Laugh lines ran from eyes that exactly matched Dillon's and Ryan's, which together with the photo in the living room, could only make him Dillon's father.

Eleanor couldn't quite meet the amusement in the smile the elder Stone turned on her as he noticed the way Ryan clung to her.

"Dad. This is Eleanor Rose…Stone."

"That wife you got by accident?"

Eleanor had the childish desire to kick her… husband in the shins. Nobody got married by accident. Except her. How could she explain it? How had Dillon explained it?

Forestalling Dillon's answer, Eleanor picked up Ryan, hugging the little boy to her for courage, then rushed headlong into an explanation as she sat, placing the willing child on her lap.

"Don't be mad. It wasn't really our fault, Mr. Stone. Jake—my foster brother—made it all sound so easy and innocent, a benefit theater dinner for a local women's shelter. Then quite by accident Dillon and I found ourselves married by the judge, who'd

made a mistake and come to the wrong wedding—''
By the time Eleanor got that far, she was breathless.

She'd never had to explain her actions to a real
live parent before, and in some bizarre way, Dillon's
dad was kind of hers, too, wasn't he? Not her very
own, of course, but as close as she was going to get.
The thought left Eleanor feeling...odd...and at the
same time elated.

''I'm not mad, girl. Dillon told me about your 'little adventure.' But since you're going to be my
daughter-in-law, you should call me Mike...or Dad,
if you'd like.''

Eleanor panicked at the hard lump that crawled
into her throat. Dad?

''You don't understand, this is only temporary. It
must look very strange to you, me living here and
everything. I had to move out of my rental and Dillon
insisted I move in with him. Well, you know, not
with him, just move in here, until I can make some
other arrangements, which I haven't been able to do.
And, anyway, Dillon has applied for an annulment,
so we can get this whole mess cleared up.'' The more
she tried to explain, the more flustered Eleanor got.
But she didn't miss the look that passed between
father and son, or the way Mike's bushy eyebrows
lifted in exact imitation of Dillon's.

As she looked from one to the other, Eleanor's
stomach twisted nervously. She'd given seminars and
spoken in front of the board of directors of her company without batting an eyelash. For goodness' sake,
she was a confident businesswoman. Why was making explanations to one smiling old gent making her
feel like she'd been a naughty little girl?

Winking, Mike caught her by surprise. "I'm sure you two will work this out. I have one daughter, but I'm glad to get another one. Been waiting a long time."

Knowing the stunned look on Eleanor's face matched his exactly—though for different reasons—Dillon couldn't believe his dad's response to the news of his and El's strange marriage.

He'd told the old man as little as he had to, but his dad had always had a different take on life. He seemed to trust the universe and the curve balls it threw at him. At an early age, he tried to teach Dillon to believe that the unexpected had meaning in his life, too. He just wasn't quite ready for the unexpectedness of suddenly finding Eleanor becoming a part of his life.

His father knew he hadn't filed for the annulment yet. That much Dillon hadn't tried to keep from him. But apparently after meeting Eleanor, his father approved.

"I have to take Pop to the airport today. He has to fly to Chicago on business. How 'bout coming with us? That way you can help me keep an eye on Ryan. He loves to watch the planes take off." Eleanor liked being with his son. He was beginning to understand how that worked in his favor.

Not surprised when Ryan hurriedly scooted off Eleanor's lap, jumping up and down in his enthusiasm, Dillon stood back and watched his son at work.

"Please, Miss Eleanor. Can we go? I want to watch Grandpa's plane fly in the air. Can we go?"

Ryan was a great equalizer.

"You don't need me to—"

"Sure we do. I want to get to know my new

daughter-in-law. I won't take no for an answer, girl.'' His dad's persuasive powers were even better than Ryan's. The old man's soft demand caused Eleanor's chiseled brows to come together in serious thought. Would she flat-out refuse?

Watching her quick mind chew on his dad's statement, something in Dillon's chest softened. He was starting to get to know Eleanor pretty well. She'd turned out to be a constant surprise to him. From experience, he knew she didn't like being maneuvered, but for some reason, she couldn't resist the challenge of the Stone men, either.

"Come on, El. Are you afraid to go the airport with us? I promise we won't gang up on you." An obvious lie, but Eleanor didn't have to know that.

She didn't disappoint him.

"Okay, rascal." She pointedly ignored him and his father as she said to Ryan, "I'll go with you, but only because you asked so nicely." The soft chuckle that escaped Eleanor at Ryan's resultant whoops pushed buttons in Dillon that had been turned off for too long.

Man, where had the need to simply hold the stubborn woman and offer her protection from the world come from, or the need to kiss her until neither one of them could think straight, or the desire to make love to her until the world stopped in its orbit for some trillion years?

Dillon didn't know what was happening, but somehow, some way, he was starting to care for the woman who was nothing like his original idea of the perfect wife. This contrary, stubborn, all-business woman turned his life upside down and was turning out to be just what his thirsty heart had ordered.

* * *

On the way to the airport, Eleanor watched suspiciously while Dillon and Ryan visited with his dad. She was sure the man was up to something. The look he trained on her in the kitchen when she'd agreed to come with them had been full of resolve and promise.

Dillon with a challenge in his eye was a hard combination to refuse. She'd already gotten into too much trouble with the impossible man. And trouble in the guise of Dillon Stone was the one thing she was determined to steer clear of.

They took her Explorer, since it was more practical than Dillon's truck for transporting family and luggage to the airport. Family. That's what Dillon had. His sister. His dad. And Ryan. Something twisted tight in Eleanor's chest and longing sprang from the painful knot. Was this what she'd missed growing up without her mother?

The thirty-minute drive to the airport was relatively easy, the light traffic making it simple for Eleanor to follow the banter between Mike, Dillon and Ryan.

When Mike included her in their conversation, his wise eyes filled with welcoming warmth, Eleanor found herself telling Dillon's dad more about herself than she intended. Against her better judgement, she felt attached to these remarkable men...and panicked. She never had a family of her own to love as it was obvious Mike loved his son and grandson.

You do have a family, an insidious voice plowed like a thunderstorm through her mind. *For a while longer, you are legally married to Dillon. That makes*

*you his wife, and Ryan's mother, and Mike's daugh-
ter-in-law.*

Stunned at the sudden, slow revelation that she honestly wanted to be Dillon's wife, Eleanor parked in the airport parking structure, desperate to do anything rather than face the feelings leaping from the Pandora's box she'd opened.

"El? Are you feeling okay?"

"Sure. I'm fine," she frantically reassured the man causing her so much turmoil.

"You look pale."

Dillon's close scrutiny made Eleanor strangely uncomfortable. A sprinkle of tremors weakened her stomach as his gaze settled and stayed on her lips. The green of his eyes darkened with a desire she was suddenly very sure she didn't want to dissect.

"I'm fine. Really. If we don't hurry, your dad's going to miss his flight," Eleanor said heading for the elevators that would take them to the airport's main lobby.

She shouldn't be here. She shouldn't be falling, minute by minute, more and more, under Dillon Stone's spell. Eleanor caught her breath and tried to reel her shaky emotions in to some semblance of order. All she had to do was stand back and let the man put his dad on the plane. Then she could take the Stone boys home and escape. Find someplace to be alone, where she could hopefully think her way out of this mess.

She knew all the reasons why love never worked for her. She just had to remember them when Dillon looked at her with smoldering passion sharpening the green of his eyes to dark emerald. Lost in planning her own preservation, Eleanor missed Mike's ap-

proach at the boarding gate, and wasn't ready for the
strong hug the older gent wrapped her in.

"Eleanor, I'm happy you're part of our family
now. I know you and the boy will work out the kinks.
You're both obviously in love. That's all that
counts," Mike said gruffly, his cheeks turning a
bright red, apparently not accustomed to giving out
this kind of advice.

Mike couldn't have surprised Eleanor more if he'd
offered her a million dollars. Still as a statue, she
watched her new father-in-law turn and gesture to
Ryan.

"Bye, champ. I'll see you next time around."
Mike ruffled Ryan's hair before quickly lifting his
grandson into a big bear hug.

"Bye, Grandpa."

Eleanor quickly blinked away the tears that stupidly surfaced at the sight of grandfather and grandson saying their goodbyes. This was what she'd been
missing all her life.

She glanced at Dillon, hoping he hadn't noticed
her sentimentality. What he had was what she
wanted. Someone who loved her enough to miss her
if she had to get on a plane and leave him behind.

You're both obviously in love.

She did love Dillon. More than life itself. She'd
been foolishly denying it, but Mike had seen the
truth. In one thing though, he was wrong. Her husband didn't love her back.

Dillon shifted restlessly in his seat as he checked
on Ryan, who had fallen asleep as soon as they'd left
the airport. He glanced at Eleanor as she drove them
home. She was too quiet...and thoughtful, her brow

furrowed slightly as she methodically wove her way through the afternoon freeway traffic.

His father, always a good judge of character, clearly liked Eleanor. What had his old man said to her when he'd hugged her goodbye? He'd been too far away to catch his father's softly spoken words, but he'd seen the look of wonder that had flooded her beautiful face. And she'd been too silent ever since.

When they got home, Dillon put his son to bed for a nap without waking the boy. Gently, he covered him with a blanket. Brushing a lock of unruly hair off the child's forehead, he thought about how much Ryan loved Eleanor. And he would bet his last dollar that Eleanor loved Ryan back.

Maybe that was one argument he could use in his defense to get her to stay. He wasn't sure he'd call what he felt for Eleanor love, but the fact that he found himself so mind-boggling attracted to the woman didn't hurt. Whatever way he looked at it, it made logical sense that they forget the annulment and stay married.

Descending the stairs, he planned to present his case to Eleanor the way he would present final arguments to a jury—thoughtful and in order. He found her standing in the middle of the living room, her back to the door holding the picture of him and his family.

Carefully, Dillon placed his hands on her slight shoulders and was rewarded by her pliant body leaning—a perfect fit—against his. He looked over her shoulder at the picture she was tracing with her pinkie.

"What did my dad say to you?" he asked, distracted by a silky strand of blond hair that tickled his chin, and the faint scent he'd come to associate with Eleanor. Dillon thought briefly of the new list folded neatly in his pocket where he'd kept it since making it the night before.

Eleanor's shoulders lifted in a soft sigh. "He said he was happy I was part of your family."

Taking the photograph and replacing it on the mantel, Dillon turned to an unresisting Eleanor. His heart clicked into overdrive at the confused, disbelieving look on her lovely face. Gently, he rubbed the frown forming between her perfect brows as he often did with Ryan.

"I am, too." Not wanting to lose an excellent opportunity to further his new goal, Dillon took advantage of this new, soft Eleanor, lowering his lips to hers.

He moved gently, inexorably trying to show her how much their attraction could work to both their benefits. If she wouldn't fight it, the feelings marching through him like Grant through Pittsburgh could go a long way toward making their marriage very workable.

When Eleanor didn't push him away, but instead stepped closer into his embrace, inviting him in, her lips parting against his, Dillon felt a rousing shout of triumph erupt, muffled only by the deepening of their kiss.

Within seconds, the only thing that mattered to him was that he was holding Eleanor in his arms and that she was holding him just as tightly back. Wanting more of her heat, he released her lips and trailed his mouth down her neck, stopping to enjoy each pulse point along the way. Eleanor's uninhibited response released Dillon's own clamoring emotions until his possessive hands moved down her backside, settling to cup each jeans-clad cheek and pull her tight against his own hard body.

"Dad..." Ryan's faint voice cut like a sharp knife through Dillon's passion.

"Dad..."

Crashing to earth from high orbit, Dillon pulled back from the brink he'd been ready to fall over with Eleanor, and was unreasonably happy to see he wasn't the only one having a hard time catching his breath. He rejoiced at the sight of the dazed look in her distracted whiskey-colored eyes.

"Uh...I'd better go get him. I guess his nap is over."

"Yeah. Whew."

Dillon let Eleanor remove herself from his hold, then watched spellbound as she gracefully sat in the overstuffed chair behind her. Her eyes clung to his...questioning.

"Dad?"

Dillon reluctantly inched toward the door.

"Maybe we can spend the afternoon looking for information on your mom and then order some pizza," he suggested, dragging his feet as he started in the direction of his son's insistent voice. He definitely didn't want to let this responsive Eleanor go.

"That sounds fine," she murmured, sounding bulldozed.

Dillon started to sizzle again at the slow, not-quite-so-satisfied smile that curved Eleanor's lips.

"Da-ad..."

"Then after we put Ryan to bed—" Dillon jerked

his head in the direction of the demanding voice growing stronger and louder "—maybe, we can…"

Desire darkened the contours of Eleanor's face, causing certain parts of Dillon's body to harden painfully.

"Maybe, we can…" The sound of sensual mischief in her voice and the hunger in Eleanor's eyes stopped Dillon dead in his tracks.

"Da-a-ad!"

Dillon took a deep breath. "Okay, I'll get Ryan. Why don't you set your laptop up in my office and we'll work in there. There's a jack and extra telephone line near my desk. Just rummage around until you find what you need."

Knowing he no longer had time to finish what he'd started, Dillon spun around and went to get Ryan. Later, he promised himself.

With that promise shining from Eleanor's smile, it was going to be very hard to keep his mind on the comfortable relationship he was thinking of bargaining for.

Eleanor went about gathering her laptop and notes from her room in a daze. She could hear Dillon and Ryan's low, laughing voices coming from Ryan's bedroom. Could this really be happening to her? Could her husband actually have fallen in love with her?

He hadn't said the *word* and she didn't have enough experience with men to know what the signs were, but she couldn't mistake the way he stared at her or the hunger that deepened the color of his gorgeous eyes. When he held her, his touch was strong and possessive. That was love, wasn't it?

Eleanor blushed, thinking about her response to Dillon's kisses. His kiss was everything she'd dreamed it would be.

Then, when he'd cradled her bottom, pulling her tight against his rugged body, he'd started a fire-cracker sizzle that began in the depths of her belly and rapidly worked it's way to her fingertips.

Was Mike right? Did Dillon have real feelings for her? "Forever" kind of feelings?

Eleanor didn't believe in love, much less trust that such an illusive sentiment was possible. Was she being given a chance to learn about trust and love with Dillon? Unfortunately, once hope was born, she didn't have the desire or strength to quash it.

When she carried her laptop down to Dillon's office, Eleanor could hear her boys in the kitchen. Leave it to Dillon to think about fixing something to eat. Smiling, the idea of the law professor taking care of her was a novelty that warmed the cold reaches of her heart, washing her in a surprising contentment. She tried to remember how she'd fed herself before she'd come to stay with him. Fast-food, that was it. Her mantra for easy living.

Making room for her computer on Dillon's desk, Eleanor quickly hooked up the necessary lines and watched as the laptop blinked to life.

Maybe two heads were better than one. Maybe Dillon with his logical lawyer's mind could help in the search for her mother.

Looking for pen and paper so she could take notes, Eleanor opened the desk drawer, only to have it stick midway. Bending to look closer, she frowned, trying to see what was making it jam. Pushing it back a little, she reached in and gingerly wiggled a file folder until it pulled loose, allowing the drawer to freely slide open.

Noticing it was labeled with her own name, vague unease skittered through Eleanor. Why would Dillon have a file on her?

Slowly, she opened the folder and found three sheets of paper. Instantly, Eleanor recognized Dillon's distinctive handwriting. Ice beginning to creep down her spine, she forced herself to concentrate as she struggled to figure out what the papers meant.

Most wanted characteristics in a wife.

Confusion deepened to anger as she read. Eleanor flipped up the first page to scan the next one.

Most likely candidates.

Locking her jaw, she read each name, the lump growing in her throat pushing aside any budding happiness that might be lingering when she got to the end without finding her own name. She should have known.

Looking from the lists to the third sheet of paper, a request for the annulment of their marriage, Eleanor tried not to jump to any conclusions. They could mean anything, she chided herself.

Focusing on the list of characteristics Dillon wanted in a wife, Eleanor fought back black pain as she read each one and realized the man she'd finally, blindly given her heart to wanted a woman for his wife that was the exact opposite of who she, Eleanor, really was.

He wanted a Suzie Homemaker. Eleanor recognized the woman Dillon had painted with words. He didn't want the woman he'd accidentally gotten stuck with. He wanted Joan. Or a woman as close to her as he could get.

Eleanor leaned weakly against Dillon's desk, her ears roaring. She realized she'd misunderstood the signs. He hadn't forgotten his late wife, the mother of his child. This mocking list proved it.

Painful tears blurring her vision, Eleanor read the last requirement on Dillon's list.

Would make a comfortable companion.

God help her. That was the one characteristic she didn't want to meet. She didn't want to be someone's comfortable companion. She wanted to take up every available space in Dillon's heart and life, the same way he did hers.

Despite all the effort she'd made not to, she'd fallen head over heels in love with Dillon Stone. Hook, line and sinker. And in the process she'd damned herself to the worst rejection of all. She could never be the woman he obviously wanted.

Suddenly galvanized, Eleanor realized she couldn't stay in Dillon's house. She had to leave. Now. Before she lost the last of any control she might have left of her shattered emotions.

But like a bad nightmare, Dillon picked that moment to block the doorway, a tray of food in his hands, a wicked smile gracing his lips.

Closing her eyes to the lie he represented, Eleanor knew there was only one way out of the painful hell she found herself in. Bluff for all she was worth. Squaring her shoulders, Eleanor vowed there was no way she was going to let Dillon Stone know just how much he'd managed to destroy her hopes and dreams.

Chapter Eleven

Spending the next few hours with temptation and having to be a gentleman around his son was going to be the most difficult thing Dillon had ever done. Remembering that hungry—and not for food—look in Eleanor's expressive eyes only spurred him on to get back to his wife as quickly as possible.

Leaving Ryan in the kitchen stirring lemonade, Dillon carried the tray he'd filled into his office. Stopping suddenly, his smile faded when he saw the look on Eleanor's face. It had taken him longer than he wanted to put together the little snack that would hold them all off until he ordered pizza.

Now the welcoming look he was expecting clanged shut like the door of a bank vault when she saw him. A look of devastation was hidden so fast he wasn't sure he'd ever gotten a glimpse of it.

Holding a file, she glared at him. Suspicion chipping at his own happiness, he hoped that file wasn't what he thought it was.

Carefully, he placed the tray on a side table. "El?"

"What's this?" she asked in a tone that could freeze an ocean.

"It looks like a file." *That was good, Stone.* Dillon shook his head at his cowardice.

"It has my name on it."

The anger building in Eleanor's voice quashed any remaining ideas of how Dillon would like the afternoon and then the evening to go. Damn.

How could he be so stupid? And how had Eleanor found the thing, anyway?

"Yeah...well—"

"What are these lists? Your idea of a joke?"

The angrier Eleanor became and the icier her tone, the more defensive Dillon felt.

"No. Sometimes I make lists when I'm trying to think. Come on, Eleanor, don't you doodle on paper when you're trying to figure something out? I make lists. It's no big deal." It was hard to keep a rein on his temper. He was a thirty-four-year-old man, for God's sake. He shouldn't have to explain himself.

"Well, it's easy to see what you were thinking about. The perfect wife for Dillon Stone. Even that saccharine contestant from the benefit dinner made the cut."

Getting Eleanor's point, Dillon hung on to his growing anger as she shook the lists almost in his face. "It's not what you think."

"No? You don't know what I think. I think you decided to get married again. But instead of finding someone just like Joan, you got stuck with me. You should have picked...that Mary. I'm sure she would have been a perfect replacement for your first wife. Oh, but I forgot. Ryan picked me, not you."

Eleanor's voice was painfully filled with sarcasm, her eyes blinking rapidly to prevent the tears building in her eyes from falling.

Shoving his hands in his pockets and watching his woman struggle with her heartbreaking emotions, Dillon swallowed the lump in his throat. Yes, *his* woman. Feeling the folded scrap of paper containing his new list, he finally realized why Eleanor's so-called faults were no longer important to him. Why he didn't mind that Eleanor left her things all over his house. Why it really didn't bother him that she only baked chocolate-chip cookies. Why his blood pressure soared every time he even thought of her. And why he missed her so much when she wasn't right by his side. He loved her. As simple as that, he loved his dating-game bride.

Why hadn't he burned those blasted lists, instead of putting them in a file that anyone could find?

The hurt etched in Eleanor's usually fearless eyes made him feel like an adolescent fool. The last thing in the world he ever wanted to do was hurt her. His fingers fiercely balling the paper in his pocket finally caught his attention. He could prove it to her. He could convince her he'd changed his mind. He pulled the new list out of its hiding place.

Eleanor barely managed to close off the crippling hurt of Dillon's rejection before she turned her back on him. Angrily, she tossed the offending file onto his desk.

"I'll have my lawyer contact yours. I want that annulment or a divorce, whichever is faster."

"El, let me explain."

"There's nothing to explain. I'm leaving,"

Eleanor said with painful resolution as she turned back to face Dillon.

At that moment, Ryan stepped out from behind his dad, tears streaming down his face. "No. You can't go," he shouted, then bolted back toward the kitchen, his pounding footsteps punctuated by the slam of the back door.

Dillon looked at Eleanor, frantic disbelief replacing his former frustration. "At least wait to go until we can talk this out."

"What's the point? I'm obviously not the woman you want. I never will be."

Turning toward the kitchen and his distraught son, Dillon remembered the list he still had wadded in his fist and stopped only long enough to lock gazes with the woman who had captured his heart.

"At least read this before you go." He thrust the paper into her unresisting hand. All he could hope for was that she would read it and understand he'd come to his senses...that he'd come to realize she was exactly what he wanted in a wife.

What else could he do or say to convince the woman that losing her would be a huge sledgehammer blow to his heart? That he would never be able to live without her.

"Wait for me." Worried about Ryan, Dillon rushed outside to find his son. It took a little while, but finally he found the little guy behind a huge hydrangea bush, squatting against the backyard fence.

"Hey, buddy. What are you doing back here?" Dillon gingerly squatted next to Ryan, who lifted his tear-stained face from little arms perched on bent knees, confirming what Dillon already knew. He felt the same way. Miserable tears brimmed in Ryan's eyes.

"I don't want her to leave."

In agreement, Dillon pulled his son close to his side. "I don't, either."

"Did we do something bad? Is that why she's mad and wants to leave us?"

"No, champ. We didn't do anything bad." *At least you didn't.* Dillon pushed away the image of those damnable lists.

"Maybe she doesn't know we love her."

Out of the mouths of babes.

"Maybe she doesn't."

"We should tell her. I don't want her to go." Ryan's chin wobbled in his determined stubbornness.

Dillon ruffled his son's hair with his knuckles. "When did you get to be so smart?"

But when Dillon carried Ryan back to the house, he knew immediately they were too late. He checked her room and his worst suspicions were confirmed.

Eleanor was gone, leaving behind only his crumpled list and the faintest scent of her perfume. The smell mocked Dillon, pointing out that he'd blown it big time. Memories washed over him. Memories of a vulnerable woman who was a survivor. A woman who had become more than his narrow idea of a comfortable wife. Who'd gone beyond being someone he'd thought he could live with and not run the risk of loving and losing, again.

He'd been wrong about Eleanor. Terribly wrong. Now, he'd realized too late he couldn't do anything else but love the impossible woman with his whole heart. She was Juliet to his Romeo. And, it seemed they were just as star-crossed as Shakespeare's young characters.

Dillon groaned. Eleanor was a survivor. She would probably do just fine without him, he thought with heartbreaking defeat. Feeling an excruciating sense of loss, he realized the real question was, could he survive without her? A loud *no* reverberated in his mind as his heart sank. He unfolded the wadded list she'd left behind, unread. No. He couldn't... wouldn't even try to live without her.

She was his life, his very breath, and he was damn well going to tell her. As soon as he could find her, he would make her listen.

Blinded by tears, Eleanor hadn't even bothered to read the ball of paper Dillon had stuffed into her hand. After tossing it on her bed, it had taken her less than five minutes to throw most of her clothes in a carryall and grab her laptop and purse. She hurried out to her car, then locked the car doors in some bizarre attempt to leave Dillon Stone and memories of her few short weeks with him behind her.

That turned her tears into watery, painful laughter. She'd worked so hard to make memories to take away with her. Now she didn't want them.

Throwing the gearshift into Reverse, Eleanor backed down the driveway, determined to put as much distance between her and that man as possible. As if he'd want to stop her, she reminded herself bitterly. He didn't want her. The lists made that painfully clear.

Her vision flooded and her heart aching, she took whatever road came next. What she had to do was get out of town fast, she admitted, defeated, knowing she'd never be able to compete with the memory of the woman Dillon still loved.

For a passing moment, Eleanor thought about trying to be the woman he wanted, but discarded the notion as quickly as it surfaced. She had her flaws, but one of them wasn't pretending to be someone she wasn't.

Wiping the moisture still clinging to her cheeks with the back of her hand, Eleanor zoomed down the highway. Dillon had called her stubborn. Pushing away the kaleidoscope of memories and searing pain where she wouldn't let them touch her, it seemed now was as good a time as any to demonstrate how right he was.

Forcing her mind to concentrate on the possible connection between Shaniko, an old boarding house and her mother, Eleanor ordered herself to stop wallowing in self pity. Life wasn't fair, and forgetting Dillon Stone was going to be an impossible task. One, she suspected, that would take more than a lifetime of unendurable heartache to accomplish. But she'd endured before. And, as always, her life *would* go on.

Dillon stood in the middle of the room Eleanor had occupied for a mere three weeks and fought the nausea that built up in his stomach. Insidiously, it linked with the panic determined to burst from his chest.

He'd put a miserable Ryan to bed more than an hour ago and still Eleanor hadn't called or returned home. Home. Where could she have gone?

Dillon slowly studied the chaotic mess of clothes and personal items that spilled from dresser drawers and the half-open closet. She'd certainly left in a hurry.

Dillon hit his fist against the doorjamb. He didn't even know where to start looking for her. He'd never met any of her friends. Didn't even think she had close friends.

It wasn't until Dillon turned to leave the unrevealing room that he remembered the unread note and noticed the diary on the nightstand, a bookmark haphazardly sticking out of its yellowed pages.

Heart constricting, he picked up the diary, looking for a clue. Carefully, Dillon turned the pages, reading as he did so, an idea—however far-fetched—forming.

He remembered Eleanor telling him Savannah Silks had owned and operated a boarding house in the early nineteen hundreds, in a small desert town in east central Oregon. Shaniko. He'd heard of it. It was mostly a ghost town now, a tourist attraction in the early stages of revitalization.

Eleanor was looking for her mother. It was possible she thought she could find the cold trail of her missing parent in this out-of-the-way ghost town. Would she head there now—without him?

He'd check the company she worked for first thing in the morning. But if she wasn't at work, his only option was to go to Shaniko and hope like hell she'd decided to go there. Somehow, he had to find her…and make her understand, despite the moronic thing he'd done, how much he loved her.

In spite of his churning emotions, Dillon slept through the rest of the night as if dead to the world.

He roused finally, to a fading dream of whiskey eyes and flowing hair the color of corn silk.

Dillon checked Eleanor's room as soon as he woke, but she hadn't returned. Everything was just as he'd left them the night before.

After making arrangements for Mrs. Holloway to pick up Ryan from school and watch the little guy until he returned, Dillon woke his son, expecting the first question out of his mouth.

"Is she here?"

"No. She's not home." Dillon hated having to tell Ryan, especially when he saw the tears begin to shimmer in his son's eyes.

"Did she die like my other mom?"

Dillon quickly grabbed Ryan, pulling his unresisting body into a hug that threatened to squeeze the child to death.

"No, Ryan. No. She just needed to take a trip." Dillon crossed his fingers behind Ryan's back, hoping he wasn't lying. "Mrs. Holloway is going to pick you up from school, while I try to find her."

"Promise you'll bring her back?"

Dillon wished he could make that promise and keep it.

"I promise I'll try, but it's up to Miss El if she wants to come home...." That word, again. It won't be home anymore without her. He had to make Eleanor understand how important she was to them...to him. Her...not some imaginary replica of Joan he'd mistakenly clung to like a fool.

Dillon dropped Ryan off at school and went straight to Eleanor's office. Thank goodness he didn't have classes for another week. She wasn't there.

She'd taken a leave of absence. So he'd have to trust his instincts and go to Shaniko.

Instincts be damned. It was the only other option he had left. He'd called the couple staying at Jake's house, just in case she'd decided to go there. But they hadn't heard from her.

It was a three-and-a-half-hour drive to the little ghost town. The sooner he got started, the sooner he'd get there...and hopefully find the woman who had taken his heart with her. He wouldn't think about what he would do if she wasn't there. He'd cross that bridge when he got to it.

Eleanor woke slowly, the warm cocoon of the quilts covering her offered a haven she was reluctant to leave. She'd arrived in Shaniko late, but was lucky enough to find a room at the Desert Motel, since the only other accommodation, the Shaniko Hotel, was already full.

Figuring she couldn't put off getting up any longer, Eleanor flipped back the warm covers and started to dress. Stoically, she pushed the painful thoughts of Dillon and the heartache that seemed to be growing, rather than diminishing, to a corner of her mind where she prayed she could keep it chained forever.

She'd lost her chance at happily-ever-after. There was only one way to spend the day, and that was not mooning over the loss of a man who didn't want her, anyway.

Eleanor had breakfast in the motel's quaint restaurant, taking her time over the omelet and toast she'd ordered. Unable to stop herself, she remembered Dillon's omelets and how much better they tasted because he made them for her. How had she let her life become so complicated?

"Have you heard of Savannah Silks's Boarding House?" Eleanor asked the waitress who'd stopped to refill her coffee. "I think it was still operating about 1905 to 1910?"

"Why, sure. That would be Tessa's Place. It's a bed-and-breakfast now, just down the street."

Eleanor instantly withdrew from the open curiosity that frankly sparkled from the woman's eyes. Betsy, her name tag read, had gray-streaked hair piled into a bun on top of her head, out of which stuck a pencil. Blue eyes twinkled as an easy smile calmed some of her jitters, reminding Eleanor how much she'd lost control of the calm, controlled woman she used to be.

"Can I get anything else for you?"

"No. This is fine, thank you." Watching Betsy as she slowly circled the dining room, Eleanor avoided thinking about what she would do next if this little town turned out to be a dead end.

Stepping out onto the old-fashioned boardwalk, Eleanor put on sunglasses to cut the sun's late-summer glare. She had them with her, but she hadn't worn her reading glasses since Dillon had accused her of hiding behind them. Was that only two days ago?

Wandering down the street, she squared her shoulders and sauntered with determined casualness in the direction Betsy had told her to go. It wasn't hard to find the bed-and-breakfast, a prettily maintained building, whose prominent sign read Tessa's Place—Proprietor Tessa Silks.

Silks?

Trying to control the sudden apprehension leaping into her stomach, Eleanor forced herself to step through the open front door. Surprised at the pretty lobby, she found herself instantly liking the country decor that made her think of a colorful flower garden. Through an open door on her left, behind the check-in counter, a woman's soft voice floated from what was obviously an office.

Needing something to do to get rid of the nervous energy twisting in her stomach, Eleanor tapped the bell resting on the counter and tried not to wish Dillon was with her.

"Just a minute. I'll be right there," a lilting voice informed her.

Eleanor waited impatiently for the woman, who she hoped would be Tessa Silks, to emerge. Long moments later, she was looking into eyes barely a shade lighter than her own. They were attached to a smiling, diminutive woman, who was inches shorter than Eleanor. Her curly blond hair fell fashionably to her shoulders.

The woman's welcoming smile instantly disappeared as her eyes widened in disbelief. "Oh," she exclaimed, and her small delicate hand rushed to cover the curves of her mouth, while tears formed in equally expressive eyes.

"Tessa Silks?" Eleanor asked shakily, unnerved by the woman's reaction.

"Yes, I'm sorry. You look exactly like someone I knew a long time ago." Tessa Silks laughed shakily and took a tentative step toward Eleanor, reaching out with one hand.

Feeling as if she were on an out-of-control roller-coaster ride, Eleanor barely found her voice. "My name is Eleanor Silks Rose. Do you know a Delilah Marie Silks?''

''She was my sister. Our mother's name was Eleanor.''

Dazed, Eleanor walked slowly back down Main Street, trying to sort out the events that spun through her head. Her first meeting with her aunt Tessa had taken most of the day. She still couldn't believe the woman hadn't turned her away.

Aunt Tessa.

Would anyone believe it? She couldn't. She had family. And if she could believe her new aunt, family that loved her...that had been looking for her for a long time.

Her mother had left a note when she'd run away from home, pregnant at sixteen. But, her aunt didn't find out about it until long after her sister's death, in a car crash shortly after Eleanor's own birth, and her parents' death from natural causes just last year.

Her aunt thought her grandparents had probably tried to find their grandbaby, but being proud and wounded by what they'd considered Delilah's fall from grace, they'd never mentioned anything about a baby to Tessa. As soon as she found her sister's note, she'd started looking, but by then it was like trying to find a needle in a haystack. Still, Tessa hadn't given up.

By the time her aunt had gotten to this part of her story, the gentle woman was holding Eleanor's hands and tears soaked both their faces.

Eleanor still couldn't believe it. Her life could have been so different. She, Eleanor Silks Rose, could have grown up with her own family to love her. She couldn't stop the wash of regret that she'd never known her mother, that Delilah had died so long ago...as alone as she, Eleanor, had spent her life.

She looked at the picture of a young Delilah her aunt had given to her. Tessa was so sure her sister had not meant to abandon her baby girl forever. She didn't know how to believe the woman, but since Delilah had died just a few days after her birth and on her way home to her family, Eleanor desperately wanted to.

''Eleanor.''

Eleanor looked up at the ragged-sounding voice, just in time to stop herself from walking straight into the solid wall of male chest that belonged to that painfully familiar voice. A flood of unwanted awareness cascaded against the fortress that crumbled instantly at the sight of Dillon Stone staring at her from behind dark sunglasses. The setting sun behind him cast his features in shadow, hiding his expression.

''What are you doing here, Dillon? How did you find me?'' Diverted by her meeting with her aunt, Eleanor couldn't stop the frightening happiness that bombarded her at the sight of her husband standing in front of her...in Shaniko...his cowboy boots planted wide, as if he had no intention of moving out of her way.

God, he looked great. Eleanor couldn't help licking her suddenly dry lips.

''I've been hunting all over for you. When I found the diary in your room, I took a chance you might have come here.'' Dillon crossed his arms over his impressive chest and just...waited.

"You've found me. So what?" Eleanor couldn't erase the hurt that suddenly came back to her.

Having trouble sustaining hot anger against the wash of pivoting love that ran over her, Eleanor looked down to hide the feelings she knew he would be able to read on her face and her eyes ran squarely into the picture of her mother.

Determined to subtract herself from the emotions raging around her heart, and wanting nothing more than to share this one special moment with the man she loved, even though he didn't love her back, Eleanor held her new treasure out to Dillon.

"I found my mother. She died right after I was born, but my aunt gave me this picture of her."

"Oh, El. I'm so sorry."

Before Eleanor knew what was happening, Dillon had her wrapped tightly in his arms as if he was never going to let her go. Surprised, she melted into his warmth—just for a moment, she promised her-self—and blinked rapidly, trying to dispatch the tears threatening her at the sympathy...and something else lacing his deep voice.

"Why were you looking for me?" Eleanor pushed against Dillon's chest but was unable to slacken his embrace. His soft denim shirt against her face muf-fled her quivering voice. "We said all there was to say. There's no point in dragging this out."

"No way, lady. You didn't read the paper I gave you, did you? I've got a lot more to say about us and our marriage and you're going to give me a chance to say it."

Eleanor pushed harder, forcing Dillon to release her.

"That isn't necessary. It's all very clear. You want

a certain type of woman—'' Seeing stubbornness set Dillon's chin, Eleanor abruptly gave in. What was the point in fighting him? Eventually, when he understood she was who she was and not who he wanted her to be, he would get it. And when he did, he would go away of his own free will.

In any case, she wasn't up to standing in the middle of Main Street having a prolonged argument about the status of their marriage. ''Okay...you've got two minutes.''

''Maybe we should do this in your room,'' the timbre of his voice deepened, wrapping Eleanor in fantasies she couldn't begin to allow and expect to come out of this encounter with her pride...and heart...intact.

''No.''

''Okay, have it your way. I made the first lists before Jake contacted me about the benefit dinner. Joan had been gone for a long time and I wanted Ryan to have a mother in his life. And I convinced myself I was ready to have a new wife in *my* life as long as I didn't do anything stupid like fall in love.'' Dillon reached out, his finger tracing a line from her temple to her chin, before continuing. ''It's been hard being father and mother to Ryan. I knew I wasn't doing a great job alone. So I thought I would look for someone I could be comfortable with, someone I could like.''

Eleanor couldn't stop the ice from cracking around her heart. Unfortunately, his stupid explanation only endeared him to her more. Who in the world would marry for a comfortable relationship so there wouldn't be any love to cause them pain?

She would, that's who, Eleanor realized, her heart

pounding so loud she was sure Dillon could hear it. If it meant she could spend every moment of her life with this man, she would do it in a heartbeat.

"Then we accidentally got married, and Ryan fell in love with you…and, all you wanted to do was get an annulment.…"

Eleanor's fragile emotions pinched painfully when Dillon mentioned Ryan's love, but didn't say he loved her, too. Could she live with that?

"So why didn't you file the annulment papers? Our marriage was a mistake and I certainly don't fit into your idea of the kind of wife you want," Eleanor reminded Dillon, still unable to look him straight in the eye.

Capturing her chin between his thumb and forefinger, Dillon removed first his sunglasses, then hers. The depth of feeling that leaped from his eyes rocked Eleanor to her core.

"No, you don't have any of the characteristics that I put on that first list—"

Anger ripping through her, Eleanor tried to break out of Dillon's hold. But, the brute only tightened his grip, making it impossible to get away.

"—but I never, ever intended to fall in love. Then you wormed your way into my life and then into my heart. And, I made a second list—a list of all the things I love about you. The one you didn't read. I love you so much, El, it hurts to think you might not feel the same way about me."

Stunned, Eleanor couldn't believe what she was hearing. "But I don't cook."

"I know."

"I don't do domestic."

"I know."

"I'm not the Suzie Homemaker you're looking for." Eleanor didn't trust the lighthearted feeling that was beginning to make her feel dizzy.

"I'm not looking for a Suzie Homemaker anymore. I have my eye on a certain working woman, if she'll have me." Dillon's gentle finger moving lightly across her parted lips effectively silenced Eleanor's next protest.

"I know all about you, Eleanor Silks Rose Stone and I love you just the way you are." Dillon pulled the battered list out of his pocket and handed it to her. "Read this. I've underlined the most important things. Our marriage was never a mistake. I want to be your husband and I want you to be my wife. Forever."

At the intense sincerity in Dillon's beleaguered expression, Eleanor's heart soared. Misty eyes made it almost impossible to focus on the list he'd handed her.

Loves Ryan.
Loves the zoo.
Makes great-tasting chocolate-chip cookies.
Would make a great mother.
Makes me want to reconsider my bachelor
    status.

God help her, she believed him. The man loved her. Why was she fighting what she'd always wanted? A big bubble of happiness emerged like the sun from the darkness of her heart.

"I have family now. My aunt Tessa. A very sweet woman, who wants me to stay for a while so we can get to know each other." Finding herself at peace for the first time in her life, Eleanor carefully folded the precious list and placed it inside her silky bra, right next to her heart. She found she liked teasing the man who was gazing at her with a look that said he'd like to kiss the living daylights out of her.

"That can be arranged. What do you say about being my real wife?" Dillon asked softly as he wrapped his arms around her once again.

"I already have a husband." Eleanor smiled, tormenting a little, sure he could read the evidence of her love in the blinding glow that was growing around her heart and the possession of the arms she wrapped securely around his neck.

"El…" he growled in warning, a smile sneaking up to his magnificent eyes.

"Okay…okay." She laughed, then told him very seriously, "I think this is our chance to grab the brass ring and run with it. I love you, Dillon Stone, more than life itself, and all I want is to spend the rest of my life being your wife and Ryan's mom."

Eleanor shrieked as Dillon instantly picked her up, one arm around her shoulders, the other under her knees as he spun her in a quick victory circle, before heading across the street to her motel.

"Where are you taking me?" she demanded, laughing.

"Mrs. Stone, I think it's time for another game of strip poker. Only this time, I'm anticipating a different ending."

Her heart soaring, Eleanor settled her cheek next to her husband's heart and happily gave herself up to his care as he carried her into the lobby of the motel. Yes, she'd come a long way from the skinny tomboy that used to follow Dillon Stone everywhere.

But her husband had it wrong. By her reckoning, winning a game of strip poker and getting to see the striptease she'd missed the last time was the perfect beginning to what was going to be the first day of the rest of their lives…together.

*   *   *   *   *

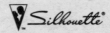

SILHOUETTE *Romance*®

COMING NEXT MONTH

#1672 COUNTERFEIT PRINCESS—Raye Morgan
Catching the Crown

When Crown Prince Marco Roseanova of Nabotavia discovered that Texas beauty Shannon Harper was masquerading as his runaway fiancée, he was furious—until he found himself falling for her. Still, regardless of his feelings, Marco had to marry royalty. But was Shannon really an impostor, or was there royal blood in her veins?

#1673 ONE BRIDE: BABY INCLUDED—Doreen Roberts

Impulsive, high-spirited Amy Richards stepped into George Bentley's organized life like a whirlwind on a quiet morning—chaotic and uninvited. George didn't want romance in his orderly world, yet after a few of this mom-to-be's fiery kisses…order be damned!

#1674 TO CATCH A SHEIK—Teresa Southwick
Desert Brides

Practical-minded Penelope Doyle didn't believe in fairy tales, and her new boss, Sheik Rafiq Hassan, didn't believe in love. But their protests were no guard against the smoldering glances and heart-stopping kisses that tempted Penny to revise her thinking…and claim this prince as her own.

#1675 YOUR MARRYING *HER?*—Angie Ray

Stop the wedding! Brad Rivers had always been Samantha Gillespie's best friend, so she certainly wasn't going to let him marry a woman only interested in his money! But was she ready to acknowledge the desire she was feeling for her handsome "friend" and even—gulp!—propose he marry *her* instead?

#1676 THE RIGHT TWIN FOR HIM—Julianna Morris

Was Patrick O'Rourke crazy? Maddie Jackson had sworn off romance and marriage, so why, after one little kiss, did the confirmed bachelor think she wanted to marry him? Still, beneath his I'm-not-the-marrying-kind-of-guy attitude was a man who seemed perfect as a husband and daddy.…

#1677 PRACTICE MAKES MR. PERFECT—
Patricia Mae White

Police Detective Brett Callahan thought he needed love lessons to lure the woman of his dreams to the altar, so he convinced neighbor Josie Matthews to play teacher. But none of his teachers had been as sweet and seductive as Josie, and *none* of their lessons had evoked passion like this!

SRCNM0603